Bad Attitude

Naima Jean

Contents

Chapter 1: An Aunt Emergency

Anywhore, Enjoy zee chapter!

(\\(•~•)/)

"What?!" I shriek, flailing my arms around. This is madness, chaos, how dare they do this to me! I sit down on the kitchen chair, holding my throbbing head with my hand.

"We won't have enough time to pick you up and take you to school and since you're not old enough to drive, we had no choice." My mother explains to me. Had no choice my ass.

"Sometimes I think you two just love to torture me." I hiss at them, making sure they know how angry I am at them.

"She's your sister, Ivory." Dad says to me. Pfft, if I had a choice I wouldn't even be related to that idiot.

"I'm your daughter, parents." I narrow my eyes at the both of them.

"Come on, it can't be that bad. It's Lavender we're talking about here!" My mom puts on a smile.

"The same daughter that ran over the neighbors mail box when she had a drivers test. The same daughter that slipped on banana peels multiple times. The same daughter that thinks I'm an overgrown sewer rat?!" I shout at them, making sure to get my point across.

"Yes, that daughter." Mom nods her head at me vigorously while I groan out at her. Ridiculous! Absolute ludicrous!

"You two are impossible." I stand up from the chair, stomping all the way upstairs. I groan the whole time I pack my bags up and all that crap.

"Hey, rat face!" Lavender shouts at me, waving her arms in the air frantically. I crunch my noise up in distaste, turning back around to face my parents.

"Oh hell no, I'm not doing this." I shake my head at them vigorously.

"Watch your mouth." My mom scolds me.

"I can't watch my mouth it's apart of my face." I roll my eyes at her.

"Smart ass."

"Wow, my ass sure does have a lot of qualities going for it today. First, it's called dumb. Now, it's called smart. People should really make up their minds." I mutter sarcastically, obviously not in the mood.

"Ivory, I hope you know that just because we're in public doesn't mean I won't take off my shoe and hit you with it." My mom glares at me and I wave my hand at her dismissively.

"Yeah, yeah, yeah." I sigh, picking up my bags and walking all the way to her doorstep.

"Not surprised to see your attitude still hasn't changed." Lavender says to me and I furrow my eyebrows at her.

"You last saw me this week."

"Oh, yeah." She racks her already empty brain probably looking for how to stop being an idiot and remember things properly.

"Idiot." I walk past her and into the house.

"Hey! I heard that." She shouts, shutting the front door.

"I couldn't care less." I smile sarcastically at her.

"Well, welcome to our humble abode!" She shouts to me, doing jazz hands. She may be an adult but, she still has the brain of a toddler.

"Looks more like a hell hole because you're here..." I trail off, setting my baggage on the ground, not caring if I hurt her feelings or not.

"Would you rather be sleeping on the sidewalk or staying here?" She raises her eyebrow at me, placing her hands on her jutted out hips. What a classic mom move.

"Do you want me to answer your question honestly or do you want me to be nice and spare your feelings?" I question her, knowing she knows that I can't be nice if my life depended on it. She groans at me, obviously irritated by my presence already.

"You're hopeless." She lets out a long sigh and I nearly laugh.

"Says the girl who couldn't even tell that her husband was falling for her in high school!" I snap at her, rolling my eyes.

"I didn't know!" She whines, stomping her foot on the ground like a little child going through a tantrum. "Besides, I could say the same thing about you!" She points at me as if she knows everything. She doesn't.

"What're you talking about?" I fold my arms over my chest, narrowing my eyes into slits at her.

"I'd love to tell you all about it but, would you look at the time..." She trails off while I continue to glare at her. "Time to go to sleep!" She pushes me into my 'new' room and closes the door.

"It's still daytime, you idiot!" I shout at her from behind the door. I groan, flopping down onto the bed and furrow my eyebrows when I see multiple beds in the room. Oh right, she actually repopulated with her husband.

I take my phone out of my back pocket, texting my friend ever since we were nine, Kaitlin. 'Guess who's staying at her sisters house whose husband is your brother?' I send to her, waiting for her to reply.

'Who?' She replies back with and I roll my eyes.

'Me!! Idiot.' I send back to her. Almost a second later I'm feeling my phone vibrate from someone calling me. I answer it, knowing who it is already.

"Since when?!" Kaitlin hollers into the phone.

"Since now." I mutter flatly.

"What's happening?" I hear Mack question from his phone.

"An emergency! An aunt emergency!" Kaitlin screeches, making me want to end the call.

"Huh?"

"Must I explain to you every time, Mack?!" She groans, taking a deep breathe of air. Oh no. "Me and Ivory's siblings have been married to each other for about 6 years and have 3 children already. They got married when they were 20 after they had Jezebel, the eldest who's 5. Which means they had Sterling a year after they were married so he's 4. They also have Shy who just turned 3. They're expecting another child soon and we're the aunt of their children." Kaitlin explains really fast, making her out of breathe when she finished.

"Why's it an emergency?" Mack questions, being able to keep up with Kaitlin's fast explanation.

"Because!" She squeals. "It means we get to see them more often since Ivory lives there now!"

"But, Kyle is your brother. You can go there whenever you like..." Mack trails off.

"Don't question me!" She shouts at him and I roll my eyes at them.

"Stop flirting you two." As if on impulse they both let out disgusted noises.

"Eww!" They shout in unison and I raise an eyebrow. Eww, I'm already turning into Lavender.

(\(•~•)/)

Chapter 2: I'm Cuter Than You

\(•~•)/)

"I brought snacks!" I hear a high pitch voice scream, running into the house uninvited. Kaitlin places the bags onto the table, trying to catch her breathe from running all the way from her house to Lavender's.

"Thank you so much, sister-in-law!" Lavender comes out of nowhere, hugging Kaitlin. Well, trying to hug her with her huge stomach. I watch in disgust as Lavender dips a pickle into the ice cream and eats it. Weird pregnant woman cravings.

"You're nasty." I scrunch up my nose in distaste.

"Don't start with me!" She points a finger at me with her mouth full as she speaks. I roll my eyes at her, not wanting to give her the time of day.

"Hey, Lavender..." Kaitlin pauses, looking around the living room before going to talk again. "Where's my idiotic brother?"

"Oh, he's still at work."

"Aren't you supposed to be at work?" I raise a questioning eyebrow at her.

"I'm pregnant." She says to me as if it's the most obvious thing in the world.

"I know that, I'm not stupid like you." I glare at her, rolling my eyes. "For your job all you have to do is take pictures. That's it."

"Do we always have to have this argument?" She sighs at me and I nod my head.

"Yes, until you convince me otherwise. I think it's the easiest thing in the world." I say.

"Photography is not only about just taking a photo, it's much more than that. You have to see-" I cut her off before she can continue her little speech.

"I don't care." I say flatly. I'm not the type of person to beat around the bush or sugarcoat things, I speak my mind. If someone has a problem with that...well, I could honestly care less if they do.

"Mom!" I hear a voice scream in the distance and I sigh, knowing what's about to happen. I watch as Jezabel of 5 years old comes stomping into the kitchen. I notice how her brown hair slightly curves at the end and how her big hazel eyes are the first thing you ever see about her.

"Yups?" Lavender questions, popping the 'p.'

"Sterling and Shy are stealing my dolls and biting on their heads!" She pouts, creating frown lines in her face.

"No I'm not!" 4 year old Sterling walks in the room with Shy wobbling and trailing after him. You're just asking for your child to hate you if you name him 'Shy.'

"If there were no witnesses in this room..." Bel trails off, giving Sterling the evil eye. Huh, I like how this girls thinks...

"No fighting." Lavender says, pouring honey on top of a pickle with ice cream on it. Nasty.

"Aww! You guys are even cuter than the last time I saw you!" Kaitlin squeals, jumping up and down. I don't get it. They look the exact same.

"That's code for I'm cuter than you, Sterling." Bel goes up to Kaitlin, letting her pick her up. She obviously loves being the center of attention and being adored.

"How rude..." Sterling mutters flatly, watching Bel stick her tongue out at him, mocking him.

"Up, up!" I look down, seeing Shy look at me with his hands in the air. "Up!" I look around the room for awhile, not knowing what to do in this situation.

"He wants you to pick him up, overgrown rat." Lavender says from besides and I turn my head, glaring at her. I carefully bend down so I'm able to pick him up. I copy Kaitlin's actions and how she's holding Bel. I awkwardly hold Shy close to me, making sure that I don't drop him.

I watch him as he puts his head on my shoulder, making me release a small smile.

"Wow, would you look at that. Ivory is capable of having emotions other than being angry and upset." Lavender comments and I roll my eyes.

"Shut your face."

"Why do you keep them all in one room?" I question Lavender, watching as she puts Shy in his crib.

"So they don't get lonely..." Lavender trails off, brushing a strand of hair away from Shy's head.

"I'd rather have my own room than sharing it with my siblings." I state, knowing they'd get tired of seeing each other every time they wake up and fall asleep.

"They're children who are scared of the dark that sleep in the dark and when they wake up they get scared. Seeing their siblings would give them comfort rather than being in an empty room that you feel unsafe and unprotected in." Lavender whispers, trying not to disturb the kids while I stay silent, taking her words in.

"I can't believe I'm saying this but, I guess you're right..." You don't know how much that sentence physically pains me to say out loud. I hear the door open from downstairs and watch Lavenders eyes get bigger, filled with happiness.

"Kyle's home!" She whisper-yells, quickly exiting the children's bedroom. I roll my eyes at how much love they still manage to hold for each other even when they're old. I walk out of the bedroom, sitting next to Kaitlin on the couch.

"Your idiotic brother is here." I elbow Kaitlin in her rib cage, catching her attention.

"No thank you." She waves her hand, continuing to stare ahead at the TV in front of her instead of coming back down to Earth. I'm not even sure if she heard me properly.

"Hey, little sis." Kyle walks up behind Kaitlin, ruffling her hair while she tries to smack him away.

"Don't ruin this for me!" She shouts, focusing on the new season of The Walking Dead. "I've been waiting for this for along time...I won't let you ruin this..." She trails off with a crazed look in her eyes and a dangerously low voice.

"Hey, Ivory." Kyle goes to raise his hand and I stop him before he can do anything.

"If you dare think to mess up my hair, I'll stuff you into the garbage disposal and shred you into tiny little pieces." I narrow my eyes into slits at him.

"Jeez, harsh crowd tonight..." He mutters under his breathe and I roll my eyes at him. The two idiots were made for each other. Kyle goes to say something and gets cut off by me and Kaitlin yelling at him.

"Shut up!"

(\(•~•)/)

Hope you guys enjoyed this chapter!

I'll try my best to upload about two-three chapters every week. Key word, try.

Xoxoxo.

Chapter 3: Madder Than The Mad Hatter

Jacob Bertrand as Mack Benjamin Day.

Ok but the first episode of TWD had me in tears.

But may my bb's Rest In peace

Enjoy the chapter!

Also, it's my b-day today ;)

(\(•~•)/)

"I really hope that Lavender has another girl. Otherwise, Jezabel would be stuck with a wild pack of monkeys." Kaitlin hums next to me.

"I just hope they stop having kids after this, for their own children's sake." I mumble loudly.

"Oh, stop being such a downer, Ivory!" I watch as Kaitlin skips into the school entrance, not caring about all the weird glances from people she's getting. One thing I don't get about Kaitlyn is how she's able to stay positive and happy twenty four seven. It drives me insane. To the brink of insanity. It makes me madder than the mad hatter.

"How're you able to stay happy all the time?" I question her, really wanting to know what her answer is. Maybe it could work for me...

"I don't know." She shrugs her shoulders. "I guess I look at all the positive things in my life!" She answers cheerfully. Well that's difficult for me. I live with Lavender now, there's no positive effect that I'll get out of it.

"Never mind." I grumble, giving up already.

"I know what you're thinking and I'm happy that you're my friend. Are you happy for something too...?" She says giving me a hopeful glance.

"I didn't ask to be your friend, you just latched onto me." I say imagining her as a blood sucking leach.

"And I'm never letting go!" She winks at me, continuing to skip throughout the halls of school.

"Whys she so happy today?" Mack questions, pointing at Kaitlin when we get to the table.

"How should I know. She's always happy. Even on Mondays." I shake my head, watching Kaitlin. What kind of sick twisted person are you if you enjoy Monday's. Much less going to school on Mondays.

"I promised you that I'd replace your necklace that Kaitlin broke when she was wearing high heels and dancing all over your room." Mack laughs softly, pulling a chain out of his bag, letting me see it. I remember that day...I had gotten ready to slice and dice Kaitlin up into tiny little pieces.

"Mack, you didn't have to replace it..." I trail off not knowing what to say to him.

"Well I did." He stretches out his hand, waiting for me to take the necklace and I do so.

"How'd you get the same exact one?" I question him in amazement.

"When you have the internet, there's nothing that you can't do." He answers simply. I mean, he does have a point that is very true.

"Want me to put it on for you?" He questions, scratching the back of his neck. I nod my head at his question, moving my hair to the side. I get a chill down my spine when I feel Mack's fingers brush up against my skin, leaving goosebumps. When I feel him put the clasp on I turn around, going to thank him until I hear a loud giggle from across the cafeteria that's almost empty because it's so early in the morning.

I lean to the side, trying to look over Mack's tall frame to see where that noise came from and see a girl with jet black hair put her hand on a guys bicep.

I look closer and recognize the face of the guy...

Zayne.

(\(•~•)/)

Sorry for the lateeee chapter! And sorry that it's so short!

I'm watching a horror movie and there's a character who has the same name as me and she honestly is the stupidest person ever.

Hope you guys enjoyed the chapter!!!!

Xoxo.

Chapter 4: Flashbacks Of The Past

Alexander Gould as Zayne Christopher Emory.

Enjoy the chapter!

(\\(•~•)/)

Zayne.

I sat in my bedroom after quickly heading down the stairs and planting the banana peels all over the ground for Lavender to step in.

For a teenage girl she really has a bad eyesight.

I watch from the top of the stairs as she sprays whip cream into her mouth, closing the fridge, and walking right into my trap. I see her fall on her butt, cackling evilly to myself.

"Are you for real?!" Lavender shouts. I let out a little giggle, walking back into my room so she doesn't get suspicious. I pick up my yearbook that I brought down, flipping to a random page and watch as my eyes lay on probably the most cutest boy ever! We would play with each other at recess. Even though his friends would mock him for playing with a fourth grader.

I sigh, tracing the hearts I drew around his framed face.

Zayne Emory.

Miss Emory.

Ivory Emory.

Nice.

"Ah ha!" Someone shouts, causing me to jump. "I got you now!" Lavender points at me, putting her hand down.

"Ok, you got me." I sigh, looking down at the yearbook.

"I knew it! I knew it all along!" Lavender does a dance around my room, playing the air guitar and failing.

"Just don't tell him I like him..." I mutter, causing Lavender to freeze in place.

"Wait what?" Lavender draws out the words.

"The boy in my yearbook." I face the yearbook towards her, letting her read his name.

"Who is he?" She furrows her eyebrows at me.

"A boy I met at recess, we played allot of games together and it was fun and all that stuff, but it's forbidden for a 4th and 5th grader to like each other." I say, watching as she bursts into laughter. She stops when she sees my serious facial expression.

"That's stupid. Why aren't 5th and 4th graders 'allowed' to like each other?" She questions me and I shrug.

"Well, it makes the upper class people look weak because they have a crush on someone younger than them." I answer her question for her in a low mutter.

"Well Ivory let me tell you something, you get your rat tail behind up off this bed and prove to those idiots that it's possible for a 4th and 5th grader to like each other. After that, I want you to kick anyone's butt who tries to get in your way. Also, don't let anyone get in your way." Lavender sends me a wink.

"Thanks Lavender, but you should really listen to your own advice." I comment, watching Lavender cock her head at me.

"What?" She's asks making me mutter 'dense.'

"I mean, the whole advice about not letting anyone get in your way. Technically, Melissa is in your way from getting to Kyle." I watch Lavender's cheeks warm up.

"T-that's a whole different scenario! Kyle's just a friend!" She stutters.

'Just a friend my butt.' I Mutter to myself in my head, watching the girl get up and leave the table that Zayne was at. I quickly fast walk over to him, pinching his ear and dragging him out into the hallway with me.

"Oww!" He whines, making me let go of him.

"What was that little scene just now?" I hiss at him, folding my arms over my chest.

"Nothing." He pauses. "What scene?" He furrows his eyebrows at me.

"The scene where you decided to let Shelby paw all over you with her hands!" I jab my finger into him.

"Ivory, you know I had to let her do that..." he trails off, awkwardly.

"Why?! Please inform me why you had to let her do it." I raise my eyebrow, waiting for him to come up with the lane excuse that he always makes.

"Because, if everyone found out that I was dating you, it'd ruin my reput ation..." He sighs, scratching the back of his neck. Called it.

"Mmm ok. So you're saying something's wrong with me." I glare at him, narrowing my eyes.

"No, nothing's wrong with you. You're absolutely perfect the way you are."

"I'm sorry for getting mad at you and assuming things..." I trail off, apologizing for the first time in forever.

"I know it's not your fault that you acted that way." He pulls me into his side, hugging me while I wrap me arms around his torso, feeling him kiss the top of my head.

(\(•~•)/)

So for those who have read 'TGWTBH' this was a reminder on who Zayne was because he didn't have a name in the other book.

Hope you guys enjoyed the chapter!

Xoxoxo

Chapter 5: The Adeline Family Tree

- -

Selena Gomez as Lavender Smith ;)

Slay, mom, slay.

Enjoy the chapter!

(\(•~•)/)

After the little hug between me and Zayne, we went our separate ways like practically every day.

"Thank god you're back, do you know how much Mack was annoying me?!" A pair of arms wrap around me, causing me to stop in my place. I raise an eyebrow as I look to the table, seeing Mack just reading a book quietly.

"He's just reading a book." I look at Kaitlin flatly when she releases me.

"Exactly. Him reading a book annoys me, so does his face." She decides to add in.

"Sometimes I worry about your mental state of mind..." I trail off.

"You're home!" Lavender squishes me into her arms, her round stomach stabbing me.

"What is it with people and hugging me today!" I snap, irritated that I'm constantly surrounded.

"I thought you wouldn't make it." Lavender releases her hold and looks at me with a serious expression on her face.

"What do you mean, 'wouldn't make it.'" I narrow my eyes at her.

"With your attitude all the time, I would've thought that you've gotten beaten to a pulp..." She trails off with a small smile on her face, shrugging.

"I'm perfectly capable of defending myself." I put my hands on my hip.

"Really now? Do you have the most powerful weapon in the world in your bag right now?" She raised an eyebrow at me.

"I do because you forced me to stick this rusty fork in my bag." I place my bag on the floor. "It was stabbing me through my bag the whole day." I sigh.

"See, you weren't prepared. You didn't correctly place it in your bag." She nods her head at me as if she knows everything in the whole world. I roll my eyes, dragging my bag all the way up the stairs to my bedroom.

"Quickly! Keep this safe away from Shy and Sterling!" Jezabel tosses me a book which I catch in the air. I furrow my eyebrows looking down at the book. Just as I'm about to ask a question she leaves the room. Great.

"Ivory!" Sterling rushes into the room, panting while holding little Shy. "Did you see Jezabel?" He takes a breathe between every word.

"Nope." I shake my head at him, popping the 'p.' I watch him grumble, walking out of the room, dragging Shy. I shake my head, opening up the mysterious book. Wow, a family wedding book. How original. I roll my eyes, looking at all the pictures in the book.

Sage and Michael Adeline.

Sage met Michael in Highschool before he came out as gay.

Lavender and Kyle Smith.

Lavender and Kyle also met in Highschool.

Violet and Alex Jones.

Violet and Alex were friends but, they started dating in Highschool. Am I the only one starting to see a pattern here? I flip the page and see my mother and father.

Dante and Esmeralda Adeline.

On a trip, my mother was visiting France and met my father. Naturally, they didn't know how to communicate with each other because they spoke two different languages. They fell in love and taught each other how to speak English. They lived happily ever after, the end. I see my aunt and uncle in the next page.

Elvira and Alejandro Garcia.

Met in Highschool, bla bla bla.

I go through the rest of the book, seeing more marriages between family members who met in Highschool. Supposedly, it's a blessing for the Adeline tree to find the love of their lives in Highschool.

You could say it's a coincidence but, when you see your whole family marry someone who they met in Highschool, you start to have your doubts that it's just a coincidence. I've had this talk multiple times with my family on how to not worry and I'll find 'the one.'

But, I have to admit...it's pretty stressful knowing to always be on alert to make sure you don't miss anyone or an opportunity or anything like that.

I sigh, closing the book, putting it aside on the table. I rub my eyes, grabbing through my backpack and pulling out a pen and some homework that I have to finish.

(\(•~•)/)

So, what do you think is up with the Adeline family tree?

Hope you enjoyed the chapter!

Xoxoxo

Chapter 6: Le Gasp!

Ansel Elgort as Kyle Smith (°□ʃ°)

Wattpad ruined my Lenny face :')

Smiling through the pain.

Also, I'm sooo sorry for the late chapter, I had so much projects stacked up on top of each other and had trouble completing them and I just got braces put on and my teeth are kinda sore.

Enjoy le chapter!

(\\(•~•)/)

"Up and early, Rugrats!" Lavender pounds the two pots together, making a loud ruckus. I groan, putting my head under my pillow to try and drown the noise out.

"Leave!" I have trouble shouting at her because my voice comes out muffled. You'd think that a pregnant woman would try to get as much sleep as she can. This pregnant woman is no normal pregnant woman, she's Lavender.

"Today is the day we eat like pilgrims and Native Americans!" She continues while I roll my eyes under the pillow. "Today is the day of the turkey, thanksgiving!" I pop my head out from under the pillow.

"I'd be thankful if you left the room and let me sleep." I narrow my eyes at her.

"There's no time for sleep! We need to get ready at 2:45 pm!" I look towards the clock and see that the time is 6:18 am.

"That's in eight hours, you idiot." I rub my eyes, knowing I have some serious eye bags under them. Stupid Lavender back at it again.

"I know that but, I have allot of stuff planned for us to do today!"

"You're annoying." I mutter flatly.

"Thanks!" She says in a cheerful tone, turning around and leaving the room.

"It wasn't a compliment!" I shout back to her, falling down onto my bed again. I look around the room and see all the kids perfectly sound asleep. When you have a parent like Lavender, I guess you get used to loud noises. I groan, turning on my side, trying to get some more sleep.

"I don't see your point." I say honestly to Lavender.

"What so you mean I don't see your point?" She furrows her eyebrows at me.

"It means exactly what I said." I give her a flat look.

"My point is that we must go to every single house in our family today."

"But why. Why can't we just call, that's too much work." I sulk, not wanting to go outside and be social.

"We can't call because it's family."

"And here we are back at the start of this conversation." I pause. "When grandma was sick in the hospital you called her, you didn't visit her."

"I was young then and I had allot of stuff going on in school..." She trails off.

"Like what?" I scoff, rolling my eyes.

"Allot of stuff." She sighs.

"Why is this situation any different?"

"It's different because you're not busy." She hums to me.

"How do you know for certain? I'm in high school and allot of teachers love to give us homework and stack projects on top of projects for us to complete." I pause. "If I fail one of my classes, just know I'm blaming you for it."

"I would be surprised if you didn't blame me for it."

I hear the front door open and close shut, making me turn to see Kaitlin fast walking over to the kitchen holding a tin-foiled-wrapped object.

"Why is the front door always open?" I raise an eyebrow at Lavender, wondering how a thief hasn't broken in yet.

"Kaitlin, why are you here so early?" Lavender questions her, voicing my thoughts out loud.

"Mom told me if I didn't get off of my behind and actually help out, she'd make me clean the whole house." Kaitlin let's out a sigh, putting the heavy object down on the table in front of us.

"That's actually being fair, with our mom she'd probably roll up the news-paper and hit us with it."

"I still remember that one day mom really wanted to slap me with her shoe." Lavender nods her head in thought.

"I wouldn't blame her."

"You were kicking my seat in the car." She glares at me.

"I was a child, I have an excuse."

"I have an excuse too."

"Really? What was it then?" I motion for her to continue.

"I was annoyed at you."

"Wow, bravo. Everyone give Lavender a round of applause." I slow clap my hands, making Kaitlin join in.

"I'm this close to dumping my pickle ice cream on both of your heads..." Lavender narrows her eyes, giving us a deadly look.

"Le gasp!" Kaitlin yells, trying to hide behind me.

"Really?" I turn around to face her.

"Yes, really! Pregnant Lavender scares me, I don't know what she's capable of." Kaitlin widens her eyes.

"What a smart girl." Lavender nods at Kaitlin.

(\\(•~•)/)

Hope you all enjoyed!

Xoxoxo

Chapter 7: I Don't Think So

A riel Winter as Shelby Roan Moon.

Ugh, I'm so sick rn.

My throat is sore and scratchy, my nose is running, and I have a 103.6 fever.

But here I am still updating

Enjoy the chapter!

(\\(•~•)/)

"But baby it's cold outside!" Kaitlin bobs her head side to side as the earphones sway with her movements.

"Do you think she'll ever stop?" Mack nudges me with his shoulder, making me focus on him.

"We both know Kaitlin, she'll never stop." I trail off with my eyes narrowed.

"Is she more annoying than how I was when we first met?" Mack sends me a small smile.

"You had an excuse, you were nine years old. Kaitlin is fifteen." I shake my head, rolling my eyes when I hear her atrocious singing again. "I bet you that she'll drop her phone in a puddle again." I hold out my hand for Mack to take.

"You're on!" Mack grins, clasping his hand around mine. We break apart when we hear Kaitlin let out a high pitched squeak, dropping her phone to the ground.

"You owe me money." I say flatly to Mack, walking behind Kaitlin. I watch as Kaitlin fishes her phone out of the muddy puddle, hearing Christmas songs blast from it even though Christmas is long gone.

"I can't believe I dropped my phone again!" Kaitlin sobs, trying to shake out water from her case.

"At least you actually listened to me and put a case on your phone." I fold my arms over my chest, rolling my eyes.

"Why me?!" She hollers, looking up at the sky dramatically.

"Why not you." I raise an eyebrow, watching her turn around and shake her head at me.

"How cruel, can't you see how much pain I am in? Have you no sympathy."

"Nope." I say, popping the 'p'.

"Come on, Kaitlin. You can just dump your phone into rice and hope that it works." Mack says trying to help, but just ends up making the situation worse.

"I have no rice at home!" Kaitlin wails, crying even harder now. I sigh really loudly, walking towards the entrance of the doors.

"Whatever. You can stay put out here if you want to catch a cold and freeze to death." I roll my eyes, shoving the doors open and start walking through the halls. I sit down at a table, putting my bag down.

I side-eye the table somewhat towards me and watch the exchange of Shelby and Zayne. He says something to her and she instantly bursts out into laughter, him joining in with her. I ground my teeth in irritation and face away from the two idiots.

"I lost my life today." Kaitlin sniffles, sitting down across from me. "All gone. All ruined." I groan, knowing she's never gonna shut up about this throughout the whole day.

"Be right back." I stand up, walking past the table and going up to the lunch line. "Can I have a napkin?" I ask the woman wearing a hairnet that's too small for her hair. She reaches behind somewhere and hand me a napkin. I turn around to start walking back to Kaitlin when I bump into someone, making me drop my binder.

"Are you kidding me." I say, glaring at the girl who bumped into me. Little miss popular man stealer I see.

"Oh my gosh," she drops down, picking up my binder and handing it to me. "I'm so sorry about that."

"Whatever." I roll my eyes, ripping my binder out of her hands as if she were fire. I knock shoulders with her as I walk past her, just to satisfy my needs a little bit to punch the living daylights out of her. I see her wince and rub her shoulder, making me smirk.

"Here." I put the napkin in front of Kaitlin's face, watching her try to dry her phone...or what's left of it.

"I see you had a little knocking with Shelby...what was that about?" Mack questions from besides me.

"Nothing." I shrug, not daring to tell anyone anything about me and Zayne. "She just bumped into me and today's not the day for me." Mack gives me a skeptical eye, not believing me and my heart starts to pick up speeds without me realizing it. I break eye contact with him and look back at Kaitlin.

"You shouldn't have danced around like a mental person, your phone would've been undamaged right now if you hadn't have done that." I rest my arms on the table and cross them.

"I couldn't help it! I'm a very bubbly person!" Kaitlin shouts, starting to cry once again for the millionth time today. "It's hard for me to stop being bubbly, that's like asking Mack to stop staring at you intensely!" She whines and I ignore the last comment she made.

"I don't do that!" Mack snaps at her, narrowing his eyes at her as if he's challenging her.

"You do! Multiple times today you've done it and you're never gonna stop!" Kaitlin narrows her eyes at him also.

"Yeah well, at least I don't take picture of the football team shirtless and plaster them all over my room for me to leave lipstick stains on them everyday!" Mack says and I eye Kaitlin.

"I-I'd never do such a thing, you liar!" Kaitlin turns the color of a ripe tomato, trying to act like an innocent angel. It's not working. "Besides, you can't use that against me when we caught you checking out the cheerleaders."

"I would never." Mack waves us off while Kaitlin turns to me and raises an eyebrow.

"You do." I nod my head at him.

"I was just appreciating their dance routines, what I can't enjoy things now?" Mack starts getting defensive and I shake my head at the two squawking birds. I turn my head and look behind me, catching Zayne's gaze. I stare back at him, not making any movement then turn my head back towards our table.

Just friends?

I don't think so...

(\(•~•)/)

Sorry for the late chapter, had allot of project to do.

Hope you enjoyed!

Xoxoxo

Chapter 8:
The Doll-Kidnapping-
Boogeyman

"What?!" I exclaim, not liking the decision that was being made. "I'm doing what now?!" I give Lavender one of my special glares when I really want to scare people.

"You are going to babysit Jezabel, Sterling, and Shy while me and Kyle go out for an adventure." She pats the top of my head as if I'm her very own dog that just does tricks for her on my free time.

"You're pregnant. I don't think you should really be going out for adventures like you're ten years old." I gave her a flat expression.

"Ivory, I feel hurt." She puts a hand on her chest as if there's actually something there. "You should remember that I am mentally a ten year old trapped inside of a twenty-five year olds body." Well, she isn't exactly wrong there.

"Why do I have to babysit them? There's a thing called 'hiring babysitter' you know." I roll my eyes at her, not believing that I can't get any alone time for at least five seconds.

"There's a thing called 'I don't have to pay you because you're my sibling' you know." Lavender fires back at me, putting a hand on her hip. 'Touché' I think to myself.

"I hope you know I'm gonna eat your favorite ice cream when you leave." I glare at her back as she turns around, getting ready to leave the room.

"I hope you know, I'm actually allot smarter than you think. I'm taking the ice cream with me." She turns her head, sticking her tongue out at me while I grimace. Once she leaves the room, I grab a pillow, putting my face into it and screaming.

I put the pillow back in it's place, knowing it won't help me one bit and yell at Lavender with my head through the crack of the door. "I still didn't willingly agree to babysitting!" I holler, knowing she's just gonna leave me here with mini hers. Disturbing and disgusting.

"Have fun!" I hear Lavender shout before the front door closes and the car starts up. I roll my eyes, letting go of a deep sigh from within me.

"Ivory-Lynn Daisy Adeline!" I look to my side and see a frustrated Jezebel, stomping her way to me while holding a teddy bear that's almost bigger than her.

"Why're you saying my full name?" Is the first thing I ask her when she makes her way towards me.

"Mommy told me to." She nods with a small smile, turning her face back into a frown. I narrow my eyes, not surprised Lavender would do that. "Tell Sterling to stop brainwashing Shy!" She stomps her foot on the ground, showing the face of her teddy bear that's covered in markers and sharpies.

"Did you do anything to make Sterling mad at you?" I raise an eyebrow at her, waiting for a response.

Jezabel puffs out her cheeks, trying to look upset when in real life she looks like a constipated chipmunk. "No." she mutters flatly. I sigh, walking into the bedroom to see what happened.

"Sterling, why did you ruin Jezabel's teddy bear." I give him a stern look, wanting to be done with this as fast as I can.

"She told me I was the reincarnation of Satan himself...then she told me I had poop breathe." Sterling pouts, looking over at Jezabel with an evil glare. These kids sure are smarter than their own parents, I know that for sure.

"Why did you call Sterling the reincarnation of Satan?" I grumble, turning my body to face Jezabel. Never thought I'd be having this conversation with little kids.

"I called him that because he said he would throw my dollies on the road for the boogeyman to kidnap them." Jezebel looks into my eyes with an innocent look. Which she does not have. No child of Lavender is innocent.

"Why would the boogeyman kidnap dolls?" I raise an eyebrow in question, wanting to know what good use of dolls would be to him.

"Let's just say he has a...wild imagination and is skillfully creativity." Sterling says, going back to teaching Shy how to divide fractions. I shake my head, walking out of the room with Jezebel.

"Are you good now?"

"Yup! Just as long as my dollies don't get thrown on the road!" She hops away with her teddy bear in her tight grasp.

"Weird kid..." I mutter under my breathe, wanting this day to be over already.

I barely flinch when the movie tries to pull another lame jump scare. I roll my eyes, sticking my head into the bowl to try and get more popcorn but, come out empty handed. I groan really loudly, sitting up and walking into the kitchen to make another bowl full of popcorn. I put a new bag into the microwave, setting it to about two minutes.

I let out a light gasp when all of the power turns off, making everything unable to see in the pitch black. I furrow my eyebrows, slowly pulling the popcorn out of the microwave. I hear a pitter-patter of footsteps running behind me.

"Hello?" I call out, obviously knowing no ones gonna answer. Come on Ivory! Horror movie 101. "Jezabel? Sterling? Shy?" My voice turns squeaky by the time I finish calling everyone's names. I widen my eyes when I see the curtain moving off in the distance. I grimace, running out of the kitchen and up to the bedroom. I look in the room and see everyone in it.

"Someone...is...downstairs..." I say each word in between intakes of breathe. I pant, watching their faces twist in confusion to shock to scared.

"It's the doll-kidnapping-boogeyman!" Jezabel breaks the silence with a loud gasp, pointing a finger towards Sterling. "You jinxed us!" She slaps him on his arm and I see him since slightly from the impact.

"I didn't know I would jinx us! I'm sorry!" Sterling cries out, looking like he's on the verge of tears.

"Sshhh! If you don't stay quiet, they'll know where w-" I suddenly get cut off with the door shaking, trying to be opened from the outside. I hear Jezabel and Sterling screech, making baby Shy start to cry. I go to the far end of the room with them huddling close to me, making me put my arms around them.

"Not the boogeyman, please! I like my dollies!" Jezabel shouts, throwing a shoe right at the door knob, making the door unlock. We all stop to glare at her while she cowards behind me, smiling sheepishly. "Oops?"

"If anyone's going first, it's gonna be you!" Sterling give Jezabel the stink eye.

"I agree!" I raise my hand up high in the air. Hey! It's fair! She's the reason for us getting thrown out the window and down onto the pavement. Technically, she's the one who killed us. We all start screaming when the door starts opening, revealing a Kaitlin with a flashlight right on her face.

"You guys should've seen your faces!" Kaitlin hunches over, grabbing her stomach and starts laughing.

"Oh, so you think this is funny?" I fold my arms over my chest, glaring at her in her hunched-over form.

"That's the reason why I'm laughing, isn't it?" Kaitlin wipes away an imaginary tear from her eye.

"How'd you manage to turn all the lights off?" I question her, deciding I'll kill her later on. I'm tired right now and want answers.

"Duh, you guys have a box that turns power on and off throughout the whole house. I just slid my arm across all the buttons so they turned off at the same time."

"You mean the fuse box...the circuit breaker?" I help her out.

"Yeah, yeah." She waves her hand, entering the room with the flashlight shining everywhere. Especially, into our eyes.

"So it wasn't the boogeyman?" Jezabel stops, looking to Sterling. "Knock on wood!" She yells, watching Sterling run over the room to find wood to knock on.

"You really gave me a heart attack downstairs." I put a hand up to my fast-beating-heart.

"Downstairs? What do you mean downstairs? By the time I entered the living room, you weren't down there." Kaitlin furrows her eyebrows, deep in thought.

"S-so...that wasn't you running across the k-kitchen?" I stutter, feeling my heart race faster.

"No?" Kaitlin says more as a question than a statement, making us all stop in our tracks.

"The-doll-kidnapping-boogeyman!" We all scream in unison, huddling back into a circle to hold each other.

(\(•~•)/)

I came up with this idea for this chapter by just simply watching a horror movie, me getting up to make soup, and the power going out while I was home alone.

But, I knew before hand the power was gonna shut off because the lights kept flickering on and off.

One of those bad storms, ya know?

Hope you guys enjoyed this chapter!

Do you guys call it a circuit breaker or a fuse box or both?

Xoxoxo!

Chapter 9: I No Longer Have An Appetite

"Hey, Lavender do you know about-" I suddenly stop talking when I fully enter the room and see what Lavender is doing.

"It's not what it looks like!" She shouts, panting.

"Dios mío, that's disgusting and disturbing!" I get a shiver down my spine just by looking at the sight in front of me.

"It's just a veggie smoothie!" Lavender shouts, continuing to drink from the nasty cup of green slush and mush.

"That looks more like insect guts squashed together and put into a drink." I crinkle my nose up at her in disgust. I watch as Lavender takes her lips off of the straw, letting the smoothie drop into the trash can.

"And now I no longer have an appetite. Thank you for that dearest sister."

"Ew, don't remind me that we're siblings. I already has to endure enough grossness today." I land on top of her bed on my stomach, spreading myself out like a starfish. "What's this whole book about?" I hand her the Adeline Wedding Family Book that I received from Jezebel earlier this week.

"Ah! This is our families special book passed on from generation to generation." She continues when I motion her to. "If you've read it already, which I know you have because you're a snooper, you can see each love has been started during high school."

"Don't you think it's a little strange that everyone in our family has met their 'soulmate' in the same time period?"

"That's where the interesting stuff comes to play. Back in the olden days things we do now were considered to be witch craft back then. They say that an Adeline just so happened to stumble across a real life witch and helped her out, for helping her she gave him a gift that no money could ever buy. True love. After that, every Adeline member has met their love in the same time period as all the others." Lavender slams the book shut out of nowhere, making me jump from being startled. "That is just a tale but, sometimes you gotta think...what if it was real..."

"How did you hear about that story?" I ask her, watching her put the book on the dresser.

"Now that I think about it, I actually don't recall anyone telling it to me..." She trails off, trying to search her mind for anything and comes up with nothing. I furrow my eyebrows in confusion, wondering how she found out about it.

"Kaitlin, has anything weird happened to you? Like something you can't really explain?" I stab the past with my fork, twirling it on the plastic plate.

"Well, at a young age I would always hum the song Fur Elise and when I say always, I mean always. I had never heard the song before like anywhere and out of nowhere I would start humming it. One day, my mom caught me humming it at and told me that my deceased grandmother loved to play that song on the piano all the time."

"Woah, that's not creepy at all..." Mack takes a swig from his water bottle.

"Has anything like that ever happened to you before Mack?"

"No. if something like that ever happened to me, my strict Christian mother would insist I was the reincarnation of the devil and have a pope perform an exorcism on me." He shrugs his shoulders, flicking his hair to one side of his head.

"Your mom sounds like an absolute lunatic." I say honestly, wondering how people can get so easily nutty.

"Ivory!" Kaitlin hisses, smacking my arm.

"What?! We were all thinking it!" I shout, flailing my arms around.

"Actually, you're right Ivory. My mother is a lunatic who likes to nag you about every little thing you do." He nods his head at me.

"Well, my mom constantly compares me to Kyle and says how he always got good grades and I don't."

"My mom left me to die on purpose with my airhead of an older sister."

"Life sucks." We all huff out in unison.

(\(•~•)/)

Short chapter.

Hope you enjoyed!

Xoxoxo

Chapter 10: Lovely Ray Of Sunshine

"Get up!" I hear momentarily before something smacks the side of my face. What a great way to start a great day. Waking up with an irritated roll of my eyes, I look above me to see who woke me up. Of course. Jezabel. Trying to calm myself so I don't lash out on her, I narrow my eyes at her.

"Why are you waking me up?" I look to my right and see the time on the clock as my left eye starts to twitch with agitation.

"Daddy has this dinner party to go to for work and we're all going with them!" She gives me a toothy grin, making me slightly more upset than happy.

"Fun."

"Lavender!" I pound on her bedroom door. "I refuse to go to a stupid party surrounded by stupid people!" I continue to pound on her door, getting louder by the second.

"You're so coming, Ivory. I need help with the kids over there and no one else is available so you can help me." She shouts from the insider of her bedroom.

"Why don't you ask one of your equally as dumb as you friends to help you?!" I glare at the door, hoping she can feel my gaze.

"They're busy." She mutters back in a flat tone.

"Well, it's not my fault you couldn't keep it in your pants for five seconds. I'm. Not. Going." I stomp all the way back to the bedroom, slamming the door shut with a loud and echoing 'thud'. I absolutely refuse to go anywhere with Lavender, letting people know that I'm the sister of that neanderthal.

"Kill me." I mutter from behind Lavender who's currently in the passenger seat.

"And here I thought I was the dramatic one, thanks for the clarification, Ivory." Lavender rolls her eyes, messing with her hair to make sure there's no loose fly-aways.

"Die." I squint my eyes at the back of her seat, folding my arms across my chest.

"We all will one day, don't worry about that." She turns around in her seat to send me a wink with a toothy grin.

"I'll be happily waiting for the day when I watch them put you six feet under ground where you can't annoy anyone anymore." I smile as I trail off, imagining the beautiful sight in my mind.

"What a lovely ray of sunshine you always are. Thanks for blessing my day with your presence." Lavender replies flatly, continuing to kick her hand, patting her hair down. When her hair flies up again for the tenth time, she releases a loud groan, closing the mirror, giving up.

"So I'm guessing you're gonna stay quiet the whole time because every time you happen to open your mouth, something dumb manages to come out." I smile in satisfaction, knowing I got the last say. I raise an eyebrow when I notice Lavender doesn't reply back with a sassy comeback. I shrug it off, looking out of the window at everything. All I know is that this is gonna suck a lot.

I watch as everyone around me has a good time, dancing and laughing. Ew. I already warded about fifteen people off by my bad attitude. It's a new record! Boy, do I feel accomplished.

"Ivory, can you watch-" Lavender comes up to me from the side, about to ask me to help her do something that I didn't want to do.

"No." I take another swig from the cup, tasting the tangy punch.

"You know it wouldn't kill you to try and be nice every once in awhile. I've seen how you treat everyone around you." Lavender gives me a look of belief.

"Oh, I'm so sorry. Maybe I would be a lot nicer to everyone if I wasn't forced to be here even though I shouted to you multiple times that I didn't want to come. But here we are now, Lavender, so what's your problem?"

"My problem is that this is something very important to Kyle and his future with this job and you're here acting like it's the end of the world. Newsflash Ivory, the earth doesn't revolve around you!"

"I know it doesn't you airhead, you don't think I realize that?! I just wonder how you don't realize that you manage to annoy every single person around you, you're annoying. No one likes you. Open your eyes and not your mouth and maybe you'd see that."

"Wow. Okay. Well at least mom and dad didn't send me away because they didn't want to have to deal with my rude attitude twenty four seven!" She retorts, making me do a double take.

"That's not what happened, you and I both know that!" I shout back, feeling a little defensive of myself.

"You sure about that because where are they right now, oh right. Gone! Poof!"

"Shut up, Lavender."

"Mom and dad were so sick of you that they dragged you onto my plate, I barely had you for two months and you're already such a drag. Can you stop for one second of your life?!"

"Shut up! We both know why I can't!" I yell at the top of my lungs, catching the attention of everyone in the party. "This is your fault, you're the one who brought me here." I point a finger at her, lowering my voice a little. Picking up my jacket that's currently draped around my chair, I wrap it around me, going outside to sit on the curb of the sidewalk.

I hate everyone.

(\(•~•)/)

Here's a chapter for you guys.

TGWTBA is finally off hold!

It feels like a breath of fresh air coming back to this book, I'm so glad I was able to get time off from it to realize how much I miss writing it.

And thank you to all of you for being so patient with me, I know how hard it was.

How do you feel about that fight that Lavender and Ivory had.

Who do you think is in the wrong?

Chapter 11: No Thanks, Hard Pass

Walking past everyone in the hallway, I go into the fridge to get a couple snacks, dragging them up with me into my room. I've been repeating this step for a couple of days now, every morning I'd get up and dig for food, going back to my room in the end.

I always managed to pick the right amounts of time to go out of the bedroom when Lavender wasn't there. Sometimes, I'd have to take sacrifices just to not see her...yeah, I'd rather not talk about that bathroom situation...

I'm perfectly happy with continuing this schedule every single day for the rest of my miserable life. I don't possibly see what could go wrong. Whenever Lavender would try to get the others to talk to me, I'd always turn them down. My attitude is a real blessing most of the times.

"Your sister wants to talk to you." Kyle comes into the room without knocking.

"Sister? I just talked to Violet the other day, what could she possibly want to talk about?!" I feign innocence, trailing off in thought.

"Harsh..." Kyle trails off, not knowing what to say and I grin, knowing he gives up.

Really it's easy to just turn people down. It's the best really. But today was different. I had to go to school today which meant I (sadly) couldn't ignore Lavender anymore. No more turning down her sad attempts of failure. No matter what I did, she'd manage to get a ride out of me and she's probably be successful.

So, not liking that idea, I made my own, I have decided to be late to school today, purposely falling behind so I don't have to talk to her. First, I'm gonna watch a movie as I snack to waste my time and then just simply leave the house once I've finished it.

Hmm, what do I feel like watching today? Something that will make me release my pent up anger. Horror is simply too perfect to pass up. Picking up the remote, I click the power button, watching the screen awaken. I click the 'horror' tab, watching endless movies pop up.

Human Centipede. No thanks, hard pass.

Bride of Chucky. Good classic, boring after you watched it a million times.

It Follows. Me, being a lazy person, am not going to watch a girl run away from something every five seconds.

This is hopeless. Absolutely hopeless.

Taking a different route, I close my eyes, randomly clicking buttons on the remote as I finally click the round circle in the middle, choosing a movie.

Are you kidding me?! Scary movie?! Who thinks that's scary? Whoever put that under the horror tab needs to be fired from their job.

Instead of changing it, I sit there, continuing to watch it with droopy eyes. Letting out a yawn, I close my eyes shut momentarily before I feel myself start to doze off.

Shoulda went with centipede.

With a quick snore, I shoot up from my spot on the bed, looking around the room with wide eyes. Did I really fall asleep? I let out a loud groan, knowing that I screwed up my plan. Glancing at my phone, I barely make out the numbers '10:51' before I stand up with my numb legs. Stupid pins and needles. Picking up my bag, I sling it around one of my shoulders, letting the other strap hang down.

Standing up, I cautiously walk outside the front door, making sure Lavender isn't anywhere around here just in case. Running onto the sidewalk, I sprint with determination. Determination to eat lunch.

Making my way into the school, I take multiple sharp turns in the hall, finally reaching my destination.

"Took you long enough!" I hear a voice shout and I turn around to see Kaitlin standing there with an angry look on her face. "Sit down missy, we need to have a little chat!" Before I can say anything else, she grabs be by my arm, dragging me onto the lunch table. "Where was you on the night before Christmas." She narrows her eyes at me, failing at doing a 'gangster' accent.

"No, that does not sound right at all." Mack says from the other side of the table, taking a bite of his food.

"Shut up, I'm the one trying here!" She leans across the table, giving Mack a loud yell-whisper.

"Continue then." Mack says. Kaitlin turns to me with her head held high, releasing a 'hmph' noise.

"Where have you been dearest Ivory." Kaitlin gives me a tight smile and I notice her left eye twitching ever so slightly.

"Up your ass and around the corner." I stand up from the table, exiting the cafeteria as I hear Kaitlin shout from behind me. Drama queen. Where the hell is he?! I continue to walk down the hallway, keeping my eyes peeled to find someone. I pick up my pace when I see a familiar build off in the distance.

"Where the hell have you been?! I kept texting you and you never responded!" Pushing into his side, I stop him from walking, making him turn to look at me.

"I have been studying for finals. Ever heard of them? They're these really hard-"

"Don't get smart with me, I know what they are." I told my hands over my chest, watching him. "You could've at least told me that you were busy and couldn't text me."

"That's the thing, I couldn't. My dad has been on my back a lot recently about getting into college and finishing high school, these few days haven't been easy on me."

"They sure as hell haven't been easy on me either but I still made time to try and talk to you." I narrow my eyes at him, getting fed up with his excuses. "You never try and make time for me anymore."

"Listen, Ivory, I need to work on my-" He gets cut off once again but not by me, by a new person in the hallway with us.

"Sorry to interrupt, but Mr. Brown would like to see us, Zayne." Shelby says from the other side of the hall, catching Zayne's attention.

"What's she doing here?" I mutter to Zayne lowly. "Is she your new girl-friend?"

"Ivory nows not the time, don't be stupid."

Stupid.

Stupid?!

He thinks I'm stupid?!

Turning on my heel, I walk away from the situation. I'll show him stupid.

(\(•~•)/)

Hope you guys enjoyed!

Chapter 12: I Might Die A Little Bit

"**M**ove." I demand from the little devil children, watching them spread like wildfire.

"Someone's moody..." Sterling trails off, not knowing what to say about the situation. No kidding.

"As mommy would say, I think it's her time of the month." Jezabel comments and in response, Shy gurgles at her.

"What does that mean?" Sterling questions her.

"It means that someone gets really mad every month. Really, really mad." Jezabel answers for him, feeling like she cracked the case.

"You all are idiots for listening to your idiot mother." I finally break, talking to them.

"We figure." Jezabel shrugs, not looking fazed at all. In a split second, they all turn on their heel, walking out of the bedroom in perfect unison. Creepy children. I refuse to believe the whole family is actually human,

Lavender was for sure made in a test tube. Who can possibly be that dumb?! Don't even get me started on the kids. Yikes.

"Do you know how hard it is to stay put under a scary bed to scare someone is?!" I hear someone mumble. Groaning, I turn around and see Kaitlin emerging from underneath my bed.

"Why must you always stalk me like this?" I question her, jutting my hip out. She's just lucky that I'm not an easily-jumpy person.

"Because..." She looks at me with a 'duh' expression on her face, despite not knowing what to say, making her trail off. "...I can..." She fails miserably.

Mentally slapping myself, I turn on my heel once again, going out into the living room. All I want is just a little peace and relaxation, why can I not even be granted with that?! I swear I'm surrounded by neanderthals that don't know anything at all! Flopping onto the couch, I pick up the remote and skim through all of the channels.

"So, what are we watching?" Kaitlin asks me, flopping down next to me.

"What am I watching. You're not staying and watching." I reply bluntly.

"Why're such a grumpy butt today?" Kaitlin pouts, pinching one of my cheeks. I quickly slap her hand away from me before she can do anymore damage.

"Aren't I always?" I narrow my eyes at the screen, getting upset at the fact that no good anything is on right now! Are you kidding me?!

"Yeah but, today it's more than usual." Kaitlin stays silent for awhile, wondering if she should say something else. Please no. "I'm just saying, you may think I'm not smart enough to catch onto anything but, Ivory I'm always here when you need to talk." Is it done yet? I watch out of the corner of my eye as she takes another breathe, opening her mouth again. Nope. "What's wrong?"

Facing Kaitlin, I make eye contact with her. "Nothings wrong, okay?! Now can you stop smothering me!" I sigh, facing the TV again. "I'm fine."

"Whatever you say." Kaitlin says skeptically, eyeing me.

"Where's Mack?" I change the subject, noticing his absence only now.

"His mother said they're doing something called a fast or whatever and she told Mack that he has to give up eating for thirty days. So he basically locked himself in his bedroom that's filled with jars of Nutella and crackers. He refuses to leave."

"That's lovely to hear." I respond positively, obviously being very sarcastic. And I thought my family were the crazy ones.

Who am I kidding?! They still are.

"Not so lovely when you get the window slammed shut on your nose. I swear he has worse mood swings than me on that time of the month." Wow, that's really saying something if it's worse than Kaitlin's.

I cock my head, turning to look at her for a little while. "You most likely deserved it."

"No! I absolutely did not!" Kaitlin squints her eyes at me, making me raise my eyebrows, waiting for her to spill the beans. She can never keep shut for more than thirty minutes. It's a proven fact. "Fine! Maybe I kind of crawled into his room when he wasn't paying attention and scared him a little but, that window hurt. A lot." She rushes out quickly, barely giving me enough time to register what just came flying out of her mouth.

"There you go, I didn't even have to talk for you to admit your wrongs this time!" I give her a tight smile, clapping really loudly, hoping I make her go deaf- partially.

"Do you have candy? I really need sugar, I'm feeling drained!" She dramatically falls back onto my bed, pretending to faint. "Seriously though, I might die a little bit if I don't get some sugar in my system."

"Last time you had sugar, Kaitlin," I put emphasis on her name, "you went around the school like a mad woman yelling about how unicorns are real and all that crazy nonsense." I remind her of that horrid day, I completely turn on my heel and walked away from her, not wanting to deal with her and her craziness that day.

"Okay, well, unicorns are real so, in your face!" She sticks her tongue out at me.

"If you stick your tongue out one more time at me, I will cut it off and turn it into soup." I warn her, watching her slowly put her tongue back inside of her mouth where it belongs. "That's what I thought."

"Can we watch a movie! Like a good movie?!" She suddenly starts bouncing on her butt, making the bed shake. "Let's watch a good movie!" She shouts in my ear, letting me know exactly what she's doing.

"Fine! Take the stupid candy!" I reach under the bed and drag out a sack full of candy, throwing it at her face, making her fall off of the bed with a 'thud'.

I watch as Kaitlin's face lights up like a Christmas tree as she digs around the bag, despite falling onto the hard floor.

"It's a miracle!" She shouts, throwing her fist up in the air thats currently filled with different varieties of candy.

I'm so gonna regret this.

Chapter 13: Yeehaw, Doggy

"Are you kidding me?! You're supposed to be the responsible and tough one here, how did she crack you?!" Mack hisses at me as he continues to watch Kaitlin at the other side of the room from the corner of his eye.

"I gave it to her because she was was annoying me." I answer him, continuing to look at her every now and then.

"She's always annoying!" Mack gives me a deadpanned stare, pointing out the obvious.

"She was especially annoying this time though." I make sure to point out to him.

"One job...just one job is all you had to do!" Mack pinches the bridge of his nose

"Look. It's not like you were here to help me, so why don't you," I point to him with a tight smile on my face, "back off."

"Did you know that there's little bugs living your eyelashes, eating away at your dead skin. They're like little friends always with you twenty-four-seven. No ones alone!" Kaitlin continues to bounce around the room a couple times for good measure.

"Too bad my mother's not here right now, we could actually use one of her prayers." Mack states ahead at Kaitlin as she repeatedly sits up and down and up and down and up...and down.

"Mommy said dinners ready." Jezabel pokes her head into the room, staring at Kaitlin with intense curiosity.

"Tell mommy I refuse to speak with her until she apologizes for what she did wrong." I glare at the wall in front of me.

"How pls do you think I am?! I can't remember that much!" Jezabel pouts, making me turn my head to glare at her. "Time of the month. I forgot." She hesitantly takes a couple of steps out of the room and sprints the rest of the way.

"Having sister problems?" Mack knocks his shoulder into mine.

"When do I never?" I pick at my fingers like it's the most entertaining thing in the world.

"I already know you're answer, but do you want to talk about it?" Mack suggests and I practically roll my eyes up into the back of my head.

"No. I don't need any of your guys pity, I'm just fine on my own. Thanks." I manage to grit out through my clenched jaw.

He shrugs. "Suit yourself."

I lift my head up, looking all over the room when I realize Kaitlin I'm currently MIA. "I think we might have a problem." Mack comments from besides me.

"No, really?!" I stand up, looking at the trail of empty candy wrappers leading out of the bedroom and into the hallway. "As if her annoyance isn't enough? She has to make a mess too!" I follow the trail, walking downstairs with Mack trailing behind me.

"Ivory, about the other day-" Someone's voice cuts through, making me intake a big breath of air.

"I'm not talking to you, and I'm especially not talking about that day." I clench my fists at my side, trying to control my anger.

"Look, I'm sorry all right-"

I cut her off once again. "Sorry doesn't mean anything! Stay out of my life before you ruin it like you've done with everyone else around you!" I shout at her, finally making eye contact with Lavender for the first time in a long time.

"Ivory!" She begins to stand up from the dinner table, trying to get to me, not before I run out of the front door. I quickly slip outside, continuing to run until I hear her stop. "Ivory!" She yells with a pant, doubling over as she puts a hand on her very big stomach.

"We need to find Kaitlin. Right now before she does anything stupid." Mack quickly jogs up to me in time.

"I'm not stupid, Mack. I know what's happening!" I snap at him before I can stop myself, not saying anything more. The quiet seems to grow stronger around us, the only sound of us panting from being out of breath.

"At least she left a very illegal pile of trash after her so we could follow her."

"Please, I hardly think that that idiot did all of this," I wave my hand towards the rubbish, "on purpose."

Mack kisses his teeth. "Touché." We slowly stop as we come to the end of the trail. "What're we supposed to do now?" He frantically moves his head back and forth as he tries to search for Kaitlin.

"It's Kaitlin, she's an easy, simple person, nothing complex...where the closest mall around here?" I ask Mack, watching him make out a map inside of his mind to get an image.

"It shouldn't be that far from here, maybe only a couple blocks." He shrugs. I take long strides forward, turning around corners every now and then until we finally reach the mall. Something simple, something simple. Mack and I split without even having to say anything.

I walk into a convenient store, looking around the aisles as I pick up a conversation from two employees that are close by me.

"Yeah, she just walked in and started talking about unicorn poop and how it's good for your skin and all that shit." The girl moping says to the other girl.

"Wow, I want whatever she's on." The other girl nods, trailing off. Candy, you imbeciles.

"Hey, have you seen a kind of short girl with dark brown hair and brown eyes." I ask the two people, tapping my foot against the floor.

"You just described half of the population of the world. You're gonna have to be a little more specific." The mop girl laughs at me, making me fold my arms over my chest.

"She acted like she was on crack." I summarize it for them, watching them both nod in unison.

"If I could remember, I think she mentioned something about riding a unicorn...whatever that means, hope that helps!" Mop girl continues to dump the mop back into the bucket, making it wet and slimy.

I turn around on my heel, walking outside as I continue to rack my brain on where Kaitlin could be.

"Yeehaw, doggy!" I hear someone shout in a horrible version of a texan accent. I spin around, watching Kaitlin as she proceeds to ride one of those little kid rides that are outside one of the shops.

Of course.

I drag my phone out of my pocket, dialing a number. "Mack, I've found her."

Chapter 14: For Your Own Good

"Tell me, Ivory, why are you here today?"

I fold my arms over my chest, narrowing my eyes at him. "I'd answer, but it seems like you already know it yourself, smart alec."

"Projection. Oldest trick in the book." He shakes his head, writing in his stupid note pad with a peaceful expression on his face.

"Not as old as your birth certificate." I scoff, not taking my eyes off of him for a second.

"How are you feeling at this moment?" He ignores me, looking up at me from his notepad.

"How are you feeling at this moment?" I retort.

"Talking about my problems, will get nowhere. It seems to me you haven't been doing so hot these couple of past weeks."

"I haven't been doing too cold either. What's the point you're trying to make?" I watch as he continues to write in his stupid book with his stupid pen and his stupid face.

"Ivory, this," He motions around the room, "will all be over with soon enough if you just communicate with me on what's going on." He gives me a hopeful look, thinking I'm finally going to give in.

"Okay..." I release a sigh. "Well, I'm feeling...I'm feeling very angry that I am here, especially with you. A complete random stranger who knows nothing about me- and I know nothing about." I look at his hand hesitating to write in his book. "Have enough space for that in your stupid book?"

"Hate to break it to you, but I have many pages to write whatever I want on it." He flips the page, scribbling on it.

"Can I leave yet?!" I groan, sliding further down the leather couch.

"Not until we solve the problem of what's going on with you recently... have you been taking your medication?"

"I don't see how any of that is you business or how that'll help me."

"Believe me, a little bit can actually go a very long way with helping people become better."

"There's no reason for me to be here right now, I'm perfectly capable of handling myself in tough situations."

"That would have convinced me you were starting to get better...if I didn't know what had happened to make you come back here. If you don't start getting better, it's gonna become a daily task for you to keep coming back here and I know how much you love that idea."

Continuing to stare at the blank wall, I finally let my eyes roam across the room. I furrow my eyes as I look on the wall to the right, seeing a bunch of different masks hanging on the wall. I look to the right, watching the bobble heads bop up and down on his desk.

"Do you have nothing left to say?" He raises an eyebrow at me, registering my body language.

"What is there left to say?" I narrow my eyes at him a little.

"If you wanna sit in here for the next hour in dead silence, that's fine by me."

"Ivory, I'll be expected to see from you soon. Today... could have gone better, but it's progress. One step at a time." He smiles at me as I stand up to walk out of the door with him trailing behind me. I send a glare Lavender's way as I walk past her.

"How did it go, Doctor?" Lavender asks worriedly as she walks up to confront him.

"It was...interesting, I'm sure you know how Ivory can get-" I cut off his sentence as I walk out into the hallway and slam the door shut behind me. Idiots. All of them. I lean up against the wall, crossing my legs over one another. I impatiently tap the wall with my finger nails, waiting for Lavender to come out.

Screw it. I push myself off of the wall, walking to the elevator as I press the lobby button. I walk straight ahead as I recognize the car. Sliding open the backseat door, I shut it close behind me as I lay sprawled out on the whole seat. Pulling out my phone, I open up Fortnite, playing on solo so I can be distracted until Lavender finally comes back.

I hear the driver door open as the game starts to lag and finally crash on me. "Ugh! Are you kidding me?!" I slap my phone on the seat, glaring outside the car window.

"Before we go home, I'm gonna have to go to the drug store and pick up some new medicine for you." Lavender mutters softly to the point where I can barely hear her.

"New?!"

"The Doctor feels as if the medicine you're taking now isn't doing any good for you...so he's giving you a different one."

"Great. More things wrong with me, that's fantastic."

"Ivory, you know I'm just trying to help you out, right?"

"You sure have a funny way of showing it... sending me off to talk to a therapist who I hardly know without my consent may I add."

"It's for your own good."

"Since when do you get to decide what's right or wrong for me?!" I raise my voice, letting my temper get the best of me.

"Since mom and dad told me to take care of you." She gives me a pointed look in the rear-view mirror. "Ivory, you might think the whole world is against you right now, but it's not... I'm trying to help you out here, I'm trying my hardest I really am...I just don't want you to end up like me."

For a couple of minutes, I take in Lavender's words. "Whatever." I mumble under my breathe quietly, going back on my phone so I can distract myself for the rest of the car ride back home.

(\(•~•)/)

Thank you guys for two-thousand reads! Honestly, I'm surprised anyone would be reading this book.

Thank you guys so so so much!

Chapter 15: Time To Get Our Party On

"**D**id any of you losers hear about the party that Marcus is throwing...tonight?!" Kaitlin bounces up and down with glee as she approaches us at our table.

"Marcus...as in Marcus Thornberry, the junior?!"

"Duh, Marcus Thornberry as in the junior." Kaitlin rolls her eyes, continuing to face me. "I overheard him talking to his friends about having an amazing party tonight that'll go down in history!"

"You do know that's a figure of speech right?" I raise an eyebrow at Kaitlin.

"More or less." She shrugs, scooping the chocolate pudding out of her cup.

"Since when do we socialize with juniors?" Mack sends me a worried glance, knowing perfectly well that we're juniors. I simply bite down into my carrot harshly.

"Since never, which is exactly why we need to step up our game and start making some changes around here! I demand it!" Kaitlin slams her fist down on the table. "And plus, this is like the most perfect day for us to go to a party...it's the weekend tomorrow." Kaitlin does a weird dance as she moves her arms back and forth. "Time to get our party on! Whoop! Whoop!"

"I'm not sure if you realize this, Kaitlin, but I have a mother that has a tracker device in my phone...to watch my every move."

"Just say you're sleeping over at Ivory's house and leave your phone at Ivory's while we go to the party."

"I guess that could work...if I actually wanted to go to that party, but since I don't, oh well." He shrugs, scraping the plastic fork against the plastic food plate.

"You're coming with or without your consent, Mack." Kaitlin hums to herself as she glance my way once again. "What about you, Ivory?"

"I guess, seeing as I have nothing better to do tonight."

"You're actually considering this?!" Mack gives me an incredulous look and I raise an eyebrow at him. "Fine," He raises his hands up in the air in surrender, "it's your guys funerals."

"So that settles it, we're going over to your house Ivory and we're going to that party! Whoop! Whoop!" Kaitlin pumps her fists in the air.

"That's not gonna get tiring." Mack mutters under his breath more to himself.

"No! Absolutely not!" Kyle glares at Kaitlin, his eyes hard with the intent of getting his point across.

"You're such a buzzkill! It's only one night, it's not like I'm signing away my soul to the devil!" Kaitlin stomps her foot on the ground, matching the glare that her brother is currently sending her.

"You might as well be! Do you even know what those..." Kyle scrunches up his nose in distaste, "boys do! They can't keep it in their pants for five seconds! You're not going to that party, end of discussion."

"That's a very hypocritical thing to say, Kyle!" She narrows his eyes at him, giving him a knowing look.

"I-We-That's a whole different story, you cant do that!" He points an accusing finger at her.

"Come on, babe," Lavender appears from the kitchen with a spatula in her hand, wrapping her arm around Kyle's waist, "they're good kids, you gotta let them have fun every now and then."

"I know that, but what if something happens to them." Kyle frowns with the idea, leaning his head on Lavender's shoulder as she rubs circles in his back affectionately.

Lavender looks our way, looking each one of us up and down from head to toe. "They're responsible, they're capable of holding their own for a couple of hours."

"Fine, they can go." Kyle groans, knowing it's best just to agree with Lavender rather than get her upset, especially with her hormones acting up and all of that.

"Yes! Hah! This is why I consider Lavender the better sibling!" Kaitlin squeals really loudly as she jumps up and down. She rushes up to Lavender, giving her a big hug. "Thank you! Thank you!" She let's Lavender go, ignoring Kyle's protests of being careful with her. "I'm gonna get ready!" Kaitlin runs back up the stairs into the room as I roll my eyes, already ready by wearing the same clothes I wore to school.

"What have I told you about cooking? I would never forgive myself if something happened to you and the baby." Kyle protectively puts a hand on Lavender's stomach.

"Paws off, I'm perfectly capable of cooking and not injuring myself, nor the baby." Lavender folds her arms over her chest at her husbands over-protectiveness.

"Good, but just incase..." Kyle pulls the spatula out of Lavender's hand as she lets out a loud groan. "I'll be taking over for the rest of the night."

"You're impossible!" Lavender stomps behind Kyle as he makes his way back into the kitchen.

"What's a party?" Jezabel sits down next to me on the couch, grasping the cloth dolls arm in her fist.

Opening my mouth, I go to answer and get cut off right before I can. Always with this family.

"You ask too much." Sterling comes out of nowhere, plopping down on the couch on the other side of me. Shy, always one step behind Sterling, comes around the couch with a pacifier in his mouth, holding a blue blanket that matches his blue pajamas.

"That's how you know I am- and will always be smarter than you." Jezabel raises her chin in the air, waiting for Sterling to reply. When he doesn't, she smiles brightly. "That's what I thought."

"Aww, look how cute you all look." Kaitlin squeals for the thousandth time today, eyes lingering on Shy. "Don't you just look adorable!" Kaitlin lightly squeezes his chubby cheek, making him blush and smile with the attention he's receiving. A ding interrupts us, I open up my phone when I see a text from Mack saying he's outside.

"Time to go!" I stand up from the couch, dragging Kaitlin behind me out of the door. Mack hands Kaitlin his phone as she quickly drops it off back inside the house. As she returns, she gets in the car, Mack driving off as soon as she does.

"Just so you know, it took a lot of persuading to let my mom borrow the car for tonight. So both of you should be very grateful, for I am your knight in shinning armor."

"More like knight in shinning undies." Kaitlin covers her mouth as she tries to stop herself from laughing out loud.

"You're a very rude person, I hope you know that." He gives Kaitlin a look of disapproval.

I continue to look outside of the window as we continue to drive to the party, as soon as we're a few blocks away from it, I can instantly hear the faint sound of the music booming, rattling the car a little bit as we get closer and closer to it.

"I feel like we're voluntarily allowing us to get eaten tonight." Mack trails off as Kaitlin looks up at the house in uncertainty.

"Come on, guys, let's go, it's probably not gonna be that bad." I step out of the car, walking on the grass to reach the entrance of the house as Mack and Kaitlin trail behind me. I quickly catch sight of someone against the wall. Turning back around to face the two, I come up with an excuse to leave. "I have to use the bathroom, stay right here." Turning back around, I make my way through the crowd on my own, not before hearing Mack's voice speak up.

"Yeah, don't mind us, just out in the open ready to get pounced and fed on!"

I slide up against the wall, next to him, waiting for him to notice my presence. I feel my blood starting to boil when he has yet to notice me. I let out a harsh cough, sending his gaze to my direction.

"Ivory! I didn't know you'd be here." Zayne's eyes widen in surprise as he looks at me.

"Yeah, well, I never really expected you to be here yourself." I fold my arms over my chest, glaring at the crowd of people instead of him.

"Listen, I've been meaning to talk to you soon, but you weren't answering any of my calls or texts..."

"I know, I was purposely ignoring them." I send him a sideway glance.

"I figured." He scratches the back of his neck, the universal signal to notify someone that they're very nervous. "Look, I'm sorry for what I said the other day, it's just school has been a real hassle on me and life's been really stressful- and you getting on my back doesn't help at all-" I cut him off before he can say anything else.

"Me?! Getting on your back?! All I wanted to do was spend a little quality time with my boyfriend, I'm sorry if that's such a crime!" I ball my fists up at my sides, finally facing him for the first time in awhile.

"Could you keep your voice down?" He whispers to me, hanging his head lowly, facing towards the ground like the coward he is.

"You want me to keep my voice down?! Trust me, Zayne, if you wanted me to become louder and involve everyone in our business, I will do so!" I raise my voice even louder this time, receiving a couple of weird glance from people. I watch as a figure comes flying into Zayne's arms out of nowhere, clinging onto him for life.

"I don't feel too good." I watch as Shelby practically collapses in his arms, not being able to stand up. Zayne sends me a pleading glance and I push myself off of the wall with a roll of my eyes, putting Shelby's arm over my shoulders, walking to the nearest bathroom.

"This conversation isn't over." I send him a fierce look, continuing to struggle as Shelby practically puts all of her weight on me.

"How much did you have to drink?" Zayne practically hollers, trying to get his voice louder than the pumping music.

"I-I only remember having one drink...then leaving it at the counter to drink it again as I was done dancing." I finally take in Shelby's appearance and notice her pale face and flushed cheeks, how she's sweating profusely, shaking like a cold chihuahua.

"I feel so...dizzy." She groans as we enter the bathroom, gently setting her down by the toilet in case she has to...do her business in there.

"Was there anyone watching your drink?" Zayne asks as he rubs soothing circles on her back as she opens the lid of the toilet, leaning over it.

"Not that I know of..." She trails off, hurling into the toilet as she violently gags into it. I watch with envy as Zayne carefully gathers her hair out of her face, holding it back for her as she continues to dunk her face in the toilet.

"You've never been that affectionate with me..." I trail off, watching how Zayne interacts with a drunk Shelby.

"Please, not now, Ivory." He sighs, brushing her hair behind her back.

"If not now, when? When will we ever have this conversation without you always cutting me off and letting me not speak?!" I shout at him, flailing my arms.

"I think it'll be best if you left." Zayne finally meets my eyes, his gaze hard and unwavering.

"Fine. I know when I'm not needed." Turning on my heel, I exit the bathroom as I slam the door behind me.

Not bothering with Mack and Kaitlin, I walk outside of the door, walking all the way back home in the lightly sprinkling rain. I open the door with a 'huff,' taking my shoes off quickly.

"How was it?" Lavender's eyes trail over my soggy hair and clothes, looking at me with confusion.

"I had a fine time."

"Don't you mean fun?" She raises an eyebrow at me and I violently shake my head.

"No, I mean fine." Gathering up the last ounce of dignity that I have, I quickly run upstairs and into the room, not bothering to change my clothes as I crawl under the cover of my bed, not able to hold myself back from sobbing into my pillow the rest of the miserable night.

(\(•~•)/)

If you thought this chapter was a roller coaster ride, get ready for the next one.

Chapter 16: Hang In There part 1

- -

I feel myself get shaken awake very violently, I sit up quickly, ready to release my wrath on whoever decided to disturb my sleep. Today was a Sunday...well it just turned Sunday...it was barely two a.m. in the morning and I already made it clear to everyone that I wanted to be left alone for awhile, this was obviously breaking my demands.

Opening my eyes, I pause as I bite my tongue back upon seeing the sight in front of me, Lavender crying and shaking uncontrollably in front of me. This is the first time I've ever seen Lavender look...so destroyed.

"Ivory," She barely manages to get my name out of her lips as she continues to shake, more tears threatening out of her eyes.

"What's wrong?" I stand up, getting out of bed as I place my hands on top of her arms to try and calm her.

"I-I don't know." She presses her hands on top of her stomach, closing her eyes as she starts to hyperventilate. "Somethings wrong..." I let my eyes travel down and see blood covering her pants. I widen my eyes as I gulp loudly.

"Lavender, try to breathe in and out...okay?" I inhale and exhale with her, trying to soothe her. "Where's Kyle?" I ask her worriedly.

"He's at work." Lavender's bottom lip quivers as she grasps onto my arms, letting out a strangled cry. "Ivory! It hurts!" I navigate Lavender's arm over my shoulders, trying to help her out of the house and into the passenger seat of the car.

"Stay right here and practicing breathing in and out like how I showed you." I grab the seatbelt, clicking it in as I strap Lavender in it. Running back inside the house, I wake all three of the kids up, picking Shy up as I head back outside, strapping them in all of their car seats.

"What's happening?" Jezabel asks, clearly shaken as she looks over at her mother who's currently groaning with pure agony.

"I don't know, Jezabel, but I'm going to do everything I can to make your mother and your siblings are safe." I say, reassuring the kid, trying to reassure myself as well as I try to remain optimistic. God, hang in there Lavender...for the sake of your life and your baby's.

"Where are we going?" Lavender hisses in pain as she holds tightly onto the door handle, making her knuckles turn white.

"To the hospital!" I shout as I close the backseat door, getting in the drivers seat.

"H-how, you don't have a drivers license or a permit!" Lavender shouts, tilting her head back as more tears pool out of her eyes.

"Does it look like that's going to stop me?!" I quickly buckle up, reversing out of the drive way, slamming on the gas pedal as soon as we're finally backed all the way out. I press my lips together in an attempt to stop myself from crying out as I see my sister suffering.

Please, don't take her away from me. I never meant those things I said to her. She's the best thing to ever happen to me, I love her. I would be nothing without her!

I plead silently to myself as I continue to speed all the way to the hospital. I park in front of the entrance doors, getting out as I look down at my feet and remember I'm barefoot. I open the door to let the kids out as they undo their own seatbelts. I make my way to Lavender's side and help her out of the car. I let Lavender lean against me as I cautiously make my way towards the entrance.

"Ma'am, you're not supposed to park there!" Someone from the distance yells at me and I simply flip him the bird, ignoring him. Jezabel carefully carries Shy as Sterling follows after her, running to keep up with us.

"Someone help!" I shout desperately at the quiet- almost empty hospital. "My sisters bleeding! Help us!" I scream louder, straining my voice, making me crack it. I let out a sigh of relief as I see nurses start to run to our direction. "You're gonna be okay, Lavender. It's gonna be okay." I whisper to her as the nurses reach us, taking Lavender away from me as they rush her down the hallway.

"Please," I grab one of the nurses arms, "save my sister and her child." I give her a pleasing look, and watch her nod her head at me.

"We'll do our best." She runs off to catch up with the others. Her words don't comfort me at all, they feel heavy on me, like a weight has been put on my chest...making me pace back and forth in the lobby as I tangle my hands in my hair.

Seven months. She's seven months pregnant, on the verge of eight mo nths...it's too early for her to be giving birth...and that blood...I swallow roughly as I throw myself into one of the nearest chairs, putting my head in my hands as I stare at the ground.

If that's not what's happening to her...then...seven months, most babies born at seven months...tend not to survive, and if the do- rarely -they will be kept in the hospitals care to hopefully keep it alive. Eight month babies...most of them survive, but that's not the case with Lavender.

If what I think is happening is happening...then that means that not only is her child's life on the line, but so is hers.

She can't die, this can't be the end for her...she's only twenty-five for crying out loud, she has the whole rest of her life ahead of her...if she goes now, she won't be able to see her kids grow up, she won't be able to grow old with Kyle, she won't be there to see me, eventually, walk down the aisle with that special someone someday.

I can't imagine my life without Lavender...it would be an absolute disaster.

Hang in there...

Chapter 17: Hang In There
part 2

I suddenly startle awake with a jump, looking at the lobby around me. I guess I must've fallen asleep. I look at the chairs around me, seeing them occupied with the three gremlins. I sigh in relief upon seeing them sleeping next to each other, sharing one big blanket.

I look down at myself as I see my body covered in a blanket. I furrow my eyebrows, not recalling ever bringing a blanket with us on the way to the hospital.

"Ivory." Someone snaps me out of my thoughts and I cautiously raise my head up, tilting it so I can see the persons face. Kyle. "There's something we'd like to show you." I nod my head as I lift myself out of the chair, wrapping the blanket around me as I stand, watching Kyle wake up the three.

"Hi, daddy." Jezabel yawns tiredly, sliding off of her chair so she can walk on the ground.

"Where's mommy?" Sterling asks with a timid voice, as if he's scared to know the answer. Kyle scoops Shy up in his arms, walking down the hallway with all of us trailing behind him.

"You'll see..." He trails off, taking multiple turns to finally end up in front of the door to Lavender's room. He quietly knocks on the door before he opens it wide open for all of us to enter. "You have some visitors." Kyle says softly with a smile on his face.

"Mommy!" Jezabel and Sterling shout in unison, both climbing on top of the hospital bed, hugging her as she laughs, holding them close to her. Shy outstretches his hands towards Lavender, closing and opening both of his fists. Kyle quickly understands, setting Shy down on top of Lavender's lap so she could hold him.

"What happened?!" Sterling suddenly shouts, making Lavender send a quiet 'shush' his away.

"Give your brother and sister the sleep they rightfully earned, Sterling." She turns her head, facing the direction of the two new additions into the family.

"You had twins?!" I whisper in utter shock, not denying the fact that I had absolutely no idea. To be fair, I just thought she was getting fatter...oops.

"Yeah." She smiles sheepishly at me. I get up on my tiptoes, trying to get a better view of them. I skim over their bands and read the names on both of them, Jacy and Shiloh. "Do you want to hold them?" Lavender smiles at me, watching me stare at them. I nod my head up at her as I watch her pick up Jacy, passing her over to me.

I pick Jacy up, taking her carefully in my arms, afraid to drop her as I hold her close to my body. "She's so tiny." I smile down at her as I look up and meet Lavender's eyes for a quick second. The three come close to the edge of the hospital bed as they try to get a better look at Jacy.

"Finally, I'm not the only girl!" Jezabel smiles at the little girl in my arms, giving her a toothy grin. "I can't wait til you're older, we're gonna dress up and play all day long." She releases a giggle.

Sterling stares straight ahead with a blank stare, "There's two of them now." He mumbles lowly.

"Sorry we're late!" Someone shouts as they slam the door open, capturing all of our attentions.

"Really Violet." I give my other older sister a pointed look, to which she sticks her tongue out at me.

"Sorry, Lavender." Violet cringes upon seeing Lavender's glare from where she rests on the bed.

"It's fine, little sister." Lavender smirks when she sees Violet's happy expression deflate.

"I told you to stop calling me that, Ivory's the baby!" She crosses her arms over her chest. Someone clears their throat from outside of the room, startling Violet. "Oh, right." She drawls our before opening the door further to reveal her childhood-sweetheart, Alex. "Now, where's my new niece."

"It's actually a girl and a boy." I sum up for her, turning my body so she can see the girl I'm currently holding. Violet tilts her head, seeing Shiloh being held by Kyle.

"How cliche, but aww!" She coos.

"We came with gifts!" Sage announces, coming inside the already crowded room with us. I stand up on my tippy-toes a bit, seeing his husband a little far behind, struggling to keep up.

"Where's mom and dad?" Lavender suddenly questions, trying to look out at the hallway for them.

"They're running a bit later than us." Sage quickly answers her.

"Poor Michael." I shake my head at Sage.

"With this crazy family, he should've known what he got himself into before marrying me." Sage quickly drops the presents and rushes back to help Michael with the rest of them.

"Let's just hope those two newbies can keep up and survive with our wacky family." Violet mumbles, looking at both of the new members.

"They're gonna need all the luck that they can get." Lavender nods her head.

"Lavender..." I mumble, pulling my legs up to my chest, resting my chin on them.

"Mhm." She mumbles, continuing to watch the TV program.

"I'm really sorry...for all that's happened in the past month. I wish I could say more, but it's hard for me to open up and explain-" Before I can continue, she gladly cuts me off.

"I understand, Ivory, I forgive you. I'm also sorry for what I said, I did not mean any of it at all." She suddenly turns to face me, grabbing both of my hands and holding them in hers. "I want you to know how much of a good person you are, even if you don't see that amazingness in yourself every time you look at yourself in the mirror." I slowly rest my head on her shoulder, listening to the words she saying to me as I slowly take them to heart. "I never want you to feel bad about yourself or ever feel alone...because I know how that feels...I'd never want to wish that upon anyone else, especially you." I smile a little, feeling something wet drip onto my chin.

Confused, I lift my chin up, touching it and looking down at my finger. Tears, huh, been awhile since I've seen those. I quickly turn my head, wiping them away quickly as if they've never happened.

The rest of the day, we all sat around in the hospital together like the big crazy family we are.

For the first time in awhile, I felt appreciated.

Chapter 18: We Need A Break

- -

"Woah," Mack whistles lowly under his breath, "looks like some-one's gotten cero sleep last night."

"You may be partially right about that." I rub my eyes together in an attempt to try and pry them open wider than they currently are. "Except, I got about a couple of hours in while sleeping in a very uncomfortable position on a hospital chair. It also doesn't help that my new medicine makes me really drowsy." I place my head on the table, yawning into my arm.

"Medicine?" Mack asks curiously and I widen my eyes slowly as I process the words I just said a couple of seconds ago. Crap! I sit there with my head in my arms, not replying to him...not knowing how to reply to him.

"Guess who's going to the winter ball!" Kaitlin shouts as she bounces over to us like a little ray of sunshine. A perfect distraction. "All three of us!" She squeals as she sits down on the table besides me.

"Kaitlin," Mack groans as he covers his face with his hands, "we told you already that we're going to only go to prom, not those other silly dances."

"Mack, you're so insulting, they're not silly...they're magical." Kaitlin stares off into the distance with a twinkle in both of her eyes. Mack quickly sends me a glance and I send one back to him.

"What about this dance is different from the other ones?" I sit up a little, hesitantly asking the question.

"This dance!" Kaitlin shouts as she stands up, holding her arms out by her sides. "This dance will be subject to all types of imagination! Anything you want, it will be guaranteed!"

"Can it buy me a plane ticket to Canada?" Mack grumbles lowly as he stabs the plastic tray of food with his plastic fork, breaking one of the tines off. Mack is obviously a big fan of Canada, I feel like most of his dreams are about him twirling around Canada like a pretty ballerina.

"No, it can't!" Kaitlin gives Mack a wide smile as she crushes his dreams in the palms of her hands. "But, it can make your dreams come true if you have a crush," Kaitlin finally sits back down, "at the dance, you'll go to this booth and you can write down your crushes name. There's endless possibilities with what you can do with them!"

"That doesn't sound too school friendly." I mutter in my arm, not knowing why I'm still listening to Kaitlin. Mack releases a snort as Kaitlin glares at us both.

"Not like that! You can choose if you want to give them an anonymous poem or if you just simply want to spend time with them in a secluded seat to get to know each other. Think about it! It's like a date just without you planning to get everything together in time! No fuss! How perfect is that?" Kaitlin sighs as she mentally goes back into her parallel dimension.

"Sounds pointless, if I wanted to get my heart broken I'd just tell my crush right here right now how I truly feel." Mack rolls his eyes at the idea of that idiotic dance.

"Well, maybe you'd get your heart broken if you have a snobby crush. My crush is a sweet, charming, and handsome dreamboat. He'd never break my heart if I told him about my feelings."

I look over and see Mack give Kaitlin a strange look, almost to say she's delusional. "Who is this crush that you fancy so much?"

"Oh, no one," Kaitlin bats her eyes, "Marcus Thornberry!" She shouts really loud, grabbing the attention of a couple of students walking by us. Kaitlin covers her mouth with her hand as she squeals, muffling it.

"Marcus Thornberry...as in the guys party who we went to the other night? You think he won't break your heart?!" Mack lets out a loud laugh, slapping his hand against the table repeatedly. "You should really get a gig in comedy."

"Haha, laugh it up. I personally know Marcus and I have proven that he is a gentle giant." Kaitlin narrows her eyes at Mack, giving him a warning.

"You know, a couple of girls got their drinks roofied at his party." I finally speak up, siding with Mack on this one.

"So?! People get roofied all the time! No big deal! Besides, it's not like it was actually him who did it."

"No one actually knows who did do it, there's a high probability it's him." I say harshly, trying to get my point off to Kaitlin.

"Also, it was his party, even if it wasn't him, it's still his responsibility." Mack comments.

"Whatever, I'm telling you guys he's sweet and innocent." Kaitlin presses, sounding like she's trying to persuade herself more than us.

"Until then, Kaitlin, focus on your schoolwork, you're not doing well in your classes at all!" I decide to change the subject, not wanting to stay on the last one. Anytime someone mentions that memory I always think of Zayne...and I don't want to think of Zayne at all, so that's that.

"I am! Stop pestering me, if I wanted to be nagged I'd go to Kyle and tell him all of my problems in life." Kaitlin groans as she thinks about her overprotective brother. The bell above us rings, making Kaitlin release another groan.

"See you guys later." I put my backpack strap over my shoulder, walking into the hall towards my class. I feel someone yank on my arm, harshly pulling me into a dark room, locking the door behind us.

"I'll give you five seconds then I'm leaving." I narrow my eyes in the darkness, knowing who it is already. I watch as he pulls a string, turning a dim light on in the small room.

"We need to talk." Zayne finally gets out after standing there awkwardly, shifting from one foot to the other.

"Funny because every time we do, it always ends up with us arguing." I turn, reaching towards the lock, ready to leave when Zayne snatches my hand, blocking the knob from me. I furiously rip my hand out of his grasp. I watch him frown as I do so. Good for him. "I'm not gonna sit here and talk to you." I turn my body again so that my back is facing towards him.

"Can you be reasonable and mature for once!" He grabs my arm, twisting my body around, putting his arm on my other shoulder.

"Stop touching me!" I rip his hands off of me as I send him a slight shove backwards. He raises his hands in surrender as I ball my hands up in fists at my sides.

"Kaitlin, I'm not gonna beat around the bush, what we have here is unhealthy," He motions back and forth between us, making me release a snort, "we need to take a break for now."

"A break?! A break so you can go hang around with Shelby without feeling guilty, knowing damn straight that you have a girlfriend who you're too embarrassed to be seen with. No, yeah, you're right we need a break." I fold my arms in front of my chest, almost to shield my heart. "We need a breakup."

"Breakup?!" He shouts, clearly confused, making me angrier than I need to be.

"You like her! Admit it! I see the way you treat her and the way you look at her! You just think I'm some dumb girl who notices nothing!" I blink quickly, trying to get rid of the tears that are threatening to spill out. "I notice everything! I notice everything, Zayne! Also, don't try and pull that 'she's just a friend' crap with me. You may think I'm stupid, but I'm not!" I lower my gaze to the ground, trying to control my breathing.

"I-I...you're right, but I still like you." Zayne tried to reach out to touch me and I take a gigantic step back and away from him. I knew it was all true but hearing him actually confirming it, it just...

"That's just not enough. If you truly liked me, you wouldn't have fallen for her."

"So that's it then?" He whispers harshly under his breath as the late bell rings.

I lightly bob my head up and down. "I need to go." Zayne finally unlocks the door and steps to the side, allowing me to leave. Without turning back, I run through the hallway doors without a care in the world.

"Hey! Get back here, you're not supposed to leave!" A security guard shouts at me. I pull my hoodie up and over my head, trying to cover my face, but mostly to cover the tears that are coming down like a waterfall.

Why does it all have to be like this.

Chapter 19: How Did That Make You Feel

A fter the day of Zayne and I's breakup, I huddled myself into a cocoon and sat like that for awhile. Partially because I just didn't want to move and because I didn't want to hear the newborns screaming at each other at the top of their lungs.

Not only were they screaming potatoes, they also were very smelly screaming potatoes- I really do not appreciate it. I should've climbed in Sage's truck and followed him home. I let my clenched fist rest upon my forehead, trying not to get myself too heated. I continue to stare angrily at the blank wall when I hear someone come into the room. Following that person is a strange smell.

I let my eyes wander over to Lavender, watching as she waves the aroma and spreads it all over the room. "Is that a sad attempt to get rid of the smell of babies?" I question her as she continues to twirl around the room like I dancer. Mental note. Refrain yourself from rolling your eyes at Lavender's ridiculousness.

"No, it's a sad attempt to try and cheer you up." Lavender suddenly stops twirling and comes closer to me, bopping her wet finger on my nose, making me scrunch it up. I rub the liquid off of my nose with my hand and sniff it.

"What in the world is this?!" I furrow my eyebrows as I look up at her for an answer. She merely bats her eyes at me and continues to spread it around the room some more.

"It's aromatherapy. Your therapist said to try this out, he thinks it might get you out of this funk that you're currently in."

This time I let myself roll my eyes at her. "I didn't mean what this is. I meant what smell." When I was in my younger stages of childhood, our mom would also use a lot of aromatherapy in an attempt to calm me down.

Lavender tosses the bottle in my lap, making me hold it up to the light to try to read it. 'Chamomile oil.'

"Chamomile is known to be an antidepressant." She plucks the bottle out of my hands as she puts it in her pocket, pulling out a completely new bottle.

"How much do you think I need." I narrow my eyes at her, noticing how full her pocket is.

"As much as you can get." She mutters as she starts spreading Cedar wood around the room. "I also have Vetiver and Lavender oil." She sends me a sly wink as I release a groan and fall back onto the bed.

"Who's watching the babies?"

"Kyle is."

"You let...Kyle watch the babies...all alone by himself?" I say slowly, watching her reaction slowly changing. Suddenly, the cry of the two sounds throughout the whole house.

"Maybe that wasn't the best decision I've ever made." Lavender cringes as the crying gets louder. She looks at me with widened eyes, "I'll be right back!", she yells as she runs out of the room.

"Move along, my minions." Jezabel shoos Sterling and Shy inside of the room with me. Jezabel slowly crawls on top of her own bed, resting her arms behind her head. "Fetch me my finest barbie doll." She waves her hand, motioning for Sterling to look inside the toybox.

"Girls are the worst." Sterling huffs out as he gets on his knees, sifting through the box.

"What did you mutter, peasant?"

"Nothing, your majesty." He picks the doll up by a thread of hair, holding it as far away from him as possible as if it's a disease. He lightly throws the doll on the bed, alongside Jezabel and flops onto his own bed. I watch with squinted eyes as they all pull out different devices, playing on them at the same time, Shy watching Sterling.

This generation. I grumble in my head as I turn my head, peering out of the window. I scoot closer to it as I watch the scenery.

"What are you looking at out there?" Jezabel asks curiously as she comes next to me, looking confused when she sees nothing outside.

"Just the clouds...and how they move and the grass swaying back and forth every time the wind picks up."

"Clouds move?!" Sterling shouts from his bed, standing up and running over to us to look out at the window.

Jezabel ignores her younger brother and furrows her eyebrows. "So you're looking at...nothing."

"Some would say that, yes. That's why you've got to use your imagination to fill in the blanks." Jezabel continues to look at me strangely and I decide to elaborate more.

"Like that cloud...it looks like a magical princess reaching down to pick up the finest of apples." I point at the window as Jezabel looks at the sky.

"Is she a magical warrior fairy princess?!" Jezabel shouts excitedly, making me crack out into a smile.

"She can be whatever you want her to be."

Shy captures my attention with his giggles and I turn around to see a disheveled Kyle standing in the middle of the hallway. "I'm never gonna be by the twins again by myself." I watch as he shakes his head, continuing to walk down the hallway. All of the kids around me let out little giggles, finding Kyle's struggles funny. Just wait until they're older and have to babysit them, bey they won't be laughing then. At the thought, I also let out a little laugh.

"What's so funny?" Jezabel tilts her head up at me.

"I'll tell you when you're older."

"Now?" She asks with a hopeful grin on her face as I let out a groan, knowing I made a huge mistake.

"Okay. The twins are finally settled down. How about we go watch some movies!" Lavender looks at the little ones, ushering them out of the room, pausing as she looks at me. "I'll be right down!" She shouts into the hallway, making her way over to me. Lavender hesitantly sits down next to me.

"What has you down in the dumps?" She drags both of her legs into her chest, wrapping her arms around them.

"Do you remember that boy I told you about when you were in senior year of high school...the one that liked me and I liked him?" I stare at my nails as if they're the most interesting thing in the world.

Lavender thinks for a second, recalling the the moment. "Yes, I do." She nods her head at me and I continue.

"Well, we kept in contact with each other throughout the years and in my sophomore year he finally decided to ask me out...and I said yes. We've been dating for about a year and a half. At least, we were." I mutter the word bitterly underneath my breath. "He basically fell in love with another girl and I suspected it for awhile, but I didn't want to break up with him. I just felt comfortable doing the same thing over and over again every year. Three days ago, I decided to finally call quits with him."

Lavender doesn't say anything for awhile, she only stays quiet as she processes my words. "So you two were in a relationship that no one knew about, right?" I nod my head at her question.

"How did that make you feel?" She asks me as I start to stumble, not finding the right words in order to answer her. "Ivory, it's okay to have human emotions." Lavender puts her hand on my shoulder and I let my eyes close.

Feel? How did that make me feel?

"I felt...like a burden, it made me feel useless, an embarrassment." I choke as I hold back a sob, not wanting to cry. I clench my fists until they both turn white. Lavender slowly places her hands over both of my fists.

"Ivory, I hope you know that you are none of those things." I say nothing else as I continue to look out of the window. Lavender says nothing either for the rest of the time being, the only thing she does is wrap her arms around me as I sob into her shoulder.

Chapter 20: My Own Definition

Once again, I had to see my therapist and actually talk to him about my feelings. Replaying the scene over and over again in my head, I realize that the more I do the more anxious I become.

It's gonna be fine. Just take a deep breath. It's gonna be okay...

Is what he told me to repeat over and over in my head again until it worked. Fake it til you make it. Somehow, that really wasn't inspiring me to tell them the whole truth and nothing but the truth.

In all of my years of life, I have never felt this antsy and shaken up. Ivory-Lynn Daisy Adeline did not get anxious from people, people got anxious from Ivory-Lynn Daisy Adeline! It's almost as if I crawled through a black hole from my cocooned blanket into a parallel universe.

Is this why people had anxiety attacks?

After walking around the room in circles multiple times, I decide to finally sit down in order to try and clear my mind up at least a little bit.

9:25. They'll be here in only a couple of minutes. Ivory, just remember what your therapist told you...

"Well, why are you so hesitant to tell them?" He asks as he furrows his brows, trying to analyze my body language as I slouch on the couch.

"I feel like they'll...not accept me."

"Well, if they do do that, Ivory, then that should be a sign to get new friends who are supportive." I mentally roll my eyes at this once again. No pues wow.

"However, if you don't tell them, you'll never really know. Just to be clear, Ivory, I'm not telling you to do anything that you don't want to do, this will only happen with your consent."

I slowly nod my head at him, processing his words. My own consent. "I'll finally tell them...sometime by the end of this week."

"Make sure you really apply a time stamp to that goal, so you don't back out of it."

Time stamp. Sometime by the end of this week.

"Is there anything else you'd like to talk about today?" He questions me as I shake my head side to side. No. "Well, I think we're done for today. See you again in a couple of weeks."

If this day doesn't go well, I think I'll be seeing him a lot sooner than a couple of weeks.

"Ivory! Your friends are here!" Lavender shouts from below, making me rush into panic mode.

9:29! I thought I had at least one more minute to try and clear my head!

I clear my throat as I stick my head out of the door. "Send them up...please!" That was also new, my therapist told me to...use polite words, so people don't think that I'm ordering them around. I'd say it's been a real struggling trying to form the words please and thank you. How are nice people never tired of being nice. I sink into my bed and wrap the covers around my shoulders, waiting for them to enter the room.

When I see their two heads bob into the room, I motion towards the end of the bed with a flick of my wrist. "Sit down...please."

"Woah, the use of the word 'please' two times in a row." Kaitlin gives Mack a look of shock, rushing over to me to shake my shoulders vigorously. "Who are you and what have you done to, Ivory?!"

I wave her hands off of my shoulders, sending her a flat glare. "Keep your paws off."

"Ooh, feisty, me gusta." Kaitlin sits on one side of the bed while Mack sits on the other side. I glare off at the wall in spite. We all sit in silence for a couple of minutes, not making any movements at all.

Mack suddenly clears his throat, interrupting our silence. "Well, great chat guys."

I slowly release a mixture of a groan and a sigh. As much as I want to tell them, I don't want to tell them. If I don't tell them now, I'm going to have to tell them even later. I have no idea where to start...do I just come out from my hiding and say it? The words I've been dreading to say for my whole life.

I know I'm not normal, but once I utter these words out loud to them both I know I'll really not be normal now. The only ones who have known about this was my family, I hadn't needed to tell them, the doctors told them. Now, I'm all on my own, I'll need to tell them with my own voice, not anyone else's.

"So...you know I have a bit of a temper on me-" before I can continue, Kaitlin cuts me off with a snort.

"A bit?!"

I roll my eyes at her as I clench my teeth. "A lot of a temper then. I don't think I've ever tried to let you guys in and fully tell you why. You see the reason for that is because...I have been diagnosed with..." I trail off, trying to find the words. O.D.D. "Oppositional defiant disorder." I fidget with my fingers, trying to remember the definition, you'd think after how many times I've read the definition over and over again, I'd be able to remember it word for word. Apparently not. "It's a disorder in children and adolescents- it is basically defiant and disobedient behavior to authority figures. That's googles definition for it, but everyone has their own opinions. My own definition for it is...something that causes you to lash out and push the ones you love the most away."

I let them sit in silence for a second, letting them go over my words to decipher in their heads. Suddenly, the silence becomes suffocating, I still haven't told the full truth yet. "And-and I guess I'm starting to show early signs of depression and I now have a therapist who I'm still iffy about and...I have some new medication to take." Once again, they still sit in silence. Please, say something.

"Who have you told other than us?" Kaitlin hesitantly asks.

"No one. You're the first ones that I'm telling. My family knew already."

"Ivory, why couldn't you have told us sooner?"

"I guess I wanted to live in a fantasy world for a little bit longer, I wanted people to see me as normal. I don't want people to walk around egg shells every time they're around me- afraid I'll might explode on them."

"Ivory," Mack says as he scoots closer to me on the bed, he gently picks up my hand and holds it in his. "You're still a normal person. O.D.D. doesn't define who you are, only you can." Funny, that's about the same words my sister Lavender said when Sage first came out to us.

"Thank you." I smile up at him sincerely, feeling the bed dip on the other side of me as Kaitlin sits next to me.

"We're here for you, Ivory. Forever and always." Kaitlin mutters as she rests her head on my shoulder.

"Promise not to laugh...do you remember in fifth grade, the kid who chased Mrs. Moxy around the campus with a stapler?"

Both of them slowly nod their head at me.

"That was actually me. The principal had to scoop me up in her arms to get me to stop chasing her. I had just gotten done getting called dumb by her- it's actually one of my triggers."

Kaitlin next to me starts to shake, trying to keep her laugh inside. Mack widens his eyes and gives her an incredulous look. Suddenly, Kaitlin bursts out laughing.

"I'm sorry, I was just remembering her face as she was screaming and running away." Kaitlin wipes some tears from her eyes, continuing to laugh.

At that, I crack a smile. "I guess it was pretty funny."

"Guess?! She sounded like a hyena, you could hear her from five blocks away!" Mack comments as he joins us, laughing.

For the rest of the day, we hung out like it was a regular day for us. It was almost as if nothing changed, as if I hadn't just spilled my deepest darkest secret. And for that, I really appreciate my friends.

Chapter 21: Two Weeks. Fourteen Days. Eight Hours.

The day was beautiful- the birds were singing and the sun was shining! Oh, please! The birds were crapping on us every chance they got and the sun was too busy being a wimp, hiding behind the stormy clouds. What a bunch of bologna! Not only was the weather ugly today, but the day until the winter ball was getting...suffocatingly closer.

It also didn't help that every time we saw Kaitlin, she'd be a timer, ticking down the dance to the last minute.

"Two weeks. Fourteen days...including the weekend. Eight hours. Forty minutes." Kaitlin mentions to us as she hops up and down, not being able to sit still for more than five seconds.

"If you don't tape her mouth shut, I will." Mack gives me an incredulous look as continues to glare at Kaitlin, hoping she'll shut up.

"Kaitlin, we have the whole school staff bugging us about it every five seconds, we don't need you bugging us too." I notify her.

"Well, forgive me, I know how you guys are with upcoming events. You should be thanking me for helping you out." She huffs out.

"Is it really considered helping if all you do is screech in our ear and drive us crazy?" Mack sighs.

"Both of you are crankier than usual today and that is neither my fault or problem."

I continue to complain and groan in my head as the line sits still, not moving even a centimeter. I watch as a certain person and their friends pop up from nowhere, cutting at the front of the line.

"Get in the back of the line! We were here first!" I yell out to them as I watch one of the boys turn around to face me.

"Make me!" He gives me an idiotic facial expression, making his friends around him laugh. I continue to walk forward, before getting stopped by Kaitlin.

"Sorry, Marcus! My friends a little cranky today, she didn't sleep very well last night! Continue on with your day!" She waves at him and smiles while he faces around again. I angrily rip my arm out of Kaitlin's grasp to glare at her.

"Really?!"

"I hope Marcus Thornberry trips and falls on his face." Mack says from besides me. "We've been waiting all this time and now we have to wait even longer because your precious pretty boy has no patience."

"Can you guys stop treating him like he's some sort of villain? He's done nothing wrong to you, you barely even know him." Kaitlin says under her breath, making Mack scoff and roll his eyes.

"Kaitlin, open your eyes, he's not a good person- I don't understand how you don't see that."

"It's my life, both of you can just get off of my back. You're not my parents. If I get hurt then I get hurt, oh well, a new life lesson." Kaitlin crosses her arms in front of her chest, staring forward, looking away from us.

I give Mack a side eye as he looks back at me for a quick second.

"We're just trying to help you." I watch Kaitlin as she stares at the back of Marcus' head.

"Both of you can stop now."

I look back at Mack, giving him a small shrug as we continue to wait in line. After what seemed like ten hours, the line started moving once again and we were quickly at the start.

"We have to get a table that's perfectly in between the food bar and the dance floor." Kaitlin turns around to inform us, pulling a paper out of nowhere with the seats and their numbers.

"Where in the world did that come from?" Mack questions as he looks back and forth between Kaitlin and the paper.

"Since the staff didn't want people to argue over the seating arrangements, they didn't hand the papers of the seats out. I do not think that is right so... I took matters into my own hands."

"Should we be scared?" Mack asks hesitantly.

"If you feel you should be." Kaitlin gives Mack an "evil" grin, scrunching her face up like the grinch.

"Nope, you ruined it." He shakes his head at her while she rolls her eyes.

"I think we should get the J table, look how perfect it is, it's practically screeching our names!" Kaitlin squeals as she bounces up and down. "I can't believe we're gonna go to the dance in two weeks, fourteen days, eight hours, and twelve minutes!"

"Oh, please take her batteries out already!" Mack looks up at the sky, waiting for a miracle to happen.

"Give it up," I pat Mack on his shoulder, "she's never going to stop!"

"Ding, ding, ding! We have a winner, ladies and gentlemen!" Kaitlin continues to mimic the sound of an alarm with her mouth as we finally walk into the room. I sigh under my breath as Kaitlin runs over to the table, bouncing up and down on her feet. They say you shouldn't give a mouse a cookie, well you definitely shouldn't give sugar to Kaitlin.

"We'd like to buy J table for three, please!" Kaitlin hollers, making the girl shrink back, covering her ears to make them stop ringing. As the girl recovers, she looks up at Kaitlin with a flat expression.

"That'll be seventy-five dollars." She holds her hand out as Kaitlin digs around in her pocket and hands the girl the money that we gave to her earlier.

The girl opens the cash register, inserting the money as she slowly rips the tickets for the three of us, handing them to Kaitlin with an annoyed look.

"Thanks!" Kaitlin rips the tickets out of her hand, running back to us with them. "Now it's official! Neither of you can try to back out now because you already spent money on it!" Kaitlin continues to laugh evilly as we finally walk out of the line.

"You say that as if we won't find another option."

"You'll try, but you'll eventually fail." She wink at Mack, making him groan as he releases she's correct. "Now all we need to do is find matching outfits!" Kaitlin wraps one around my shoulders and her other around Mack's, squeezing us together. "This is gonna be a perfect night!"

(\\(•~•)/)

Wow, it feels like I haven't to you guys in awhile. So sorry about that!

I was originally planning to wrap this book up around Summer, but I had to take some classes during summer school in order to get spanish this year. So yea that was something.

Sorry for suuuuch a long wait for this chapter, and for some who read TQOD, sorry for not uploading that.

My first day of school was on August 7th and that didn't give me as much time as I would've liked to be able to write these chapters.

On top of that, I had to wait four weeks for the councilor to change my schedule because I was placed in the wrong math class because my school is so great at communicating ._.

Anyways, I am almost finished with this book, I'm taking a guess that there's gonna be about... four to six chapters left.

Start the countdown, ladies and gentlemen! This book is almost done!

Thank you for following me this far on this journey!

xoxoxo~

Chapter 22: Head Over Heels

"Okay, no, this back isn't doing it for me." I was currently in a dressing room with Kaitlin as we both tried on multiple dresses at the same time. I wasn't planning on the weekend going this way, but my therapist had recommended me to get some fresh air and we somehow ended up here. "Kaitlin, can you loosen up the lace?" I asked her as I turned away from the corner, facing Kaitlin's back.

"Yes! As long as you help me into this skin tight dress afterwords." She turns around, awkwardly walking towards me in the tight dress to my back.

"Why do you want such a tight dress? I know you're gonna want to be eating a lot when we're at the dance."

"Can a girl not wear a really tight dress that literally takes their breath away?" She asks as she unravels the lace, putting the dress straps up and over my shoulders.

"If you wanted to have your breath taken away, you could've just asked Mack, he could've suffocated you with his pillow earlier." I look in the mirror that was provided in the dressing room, twisting my body to get a better look at the dress. I scrunch my nose up at it. "This is why I hate shopping!" I groan as I step out of the dress, picking up the hangar as I put it back up. I step back into my regular clothes before helping Kaitlin into her breath-taking- dress.

"This was a mistake, I can't do this." Kaitlin wheezes in the dress, barely able to breath. "Ivory, get me out of here right now!" She shouts at me as she raises her arms in the air. I grab the top of the dress, trying to yank it up and over her head.

"It's not coming off!" I let go as Kaitlin starts to panic, running around the small dressing room like a chicken who just got its head cut off.

"No, no, no! Ivory, why did you let me try on this dress?!" She shouts as she continues to run around, making me narrow my eyes at her.

"I was the one who suggested you to not wear it." She suddenly pauses, thinking back.

"Oh, yeah, but you know my brain can't function properly when I'm in a stressful situation like this!" Kaitlin starts to hyperventilate as she runs around the room once again. "What if I never get out of this?! I'll be forced to go to the dance like this, It'll by my wedding day and I'll have to get married to Marcus in this dress. Hell, I'll be in the hospital giving birth with this dress on! I'm doomed for all of eternity!" She dramatically falls to her knees, looking up at the ceiling.

I roll my eyes at her before walking up behind her, grabbing the dress once again and tugging it straight upwards, finally able to get it off of Kaitlin's body.

Kaitlin releases a blissful sigh, falling to the ground as she wraps her arms around herself. "Being fat never felt better."

I gather her regular clothes up in my arms, flying them on top of her partially-naked body. "Hurry up and change so we can hang these dresses back up." I cross my arms over my chest as I watch her crawl around the floor like a newborn puppy, still dramatically gasping for air as she puts her clothes back on.

I open the dressing room, walking out of it with four of the dresses I chose in my arms. Kaitlin trails behind me with a thousand dresses in her arms, making it look like they're all swallowing her. As we head back to the racks we were just at around ten minutes ago, we place all of our dresses back on top of it with a huff.

"Why did we agree to do this again?!" Mack appears besides us, equally as out of breath as Kaitlin is.

"Because Kaitlin is annoying whenever we say 'no' to her." I cross my arms over my chest as I walk over to a new section of dresses that we haven't seen before.

"I hope you two know that I love you two dearly, but never will I ever wear matching outfits with you guys to the dance." Mack's eyes flicker between Kaitlin and I, lingering on me.

"Deal." I offer him my hand, watching him shake it.

"No, I said we were gonna match and that's final." Kaitlin interrupts our handshake, slapping our hands away from each other.

"I already said no, I don't know how you're gonna be able to get me into a matching suit." Mack challenges Kaitlin.

"Oh, please, you're the weakest and least intimidating thing in this store." Kaitlin snorts as she continues to sift through the rack.

"Okay, point taken. What about Ivory, then?" Mack points to me, making Kaitlin widen her eyes.

"Ivory's a different story, I don't know how, but I'll do it. And by me, I mean I'll hire someone to do it. I'd never put my hands on top of Ivory when she's upset." Kaitlin gives Mack a sheepish smile as she continues to look through the dresses.

"Wow, it's like I'm totally not standing here right now." I roll my eyes as I head to another row, looking in between racks. Mack slowly approaches me from the side, talking under his breath.

"I'm kinda worried about Kaitlin..." He trails off as he watches her look through the dresses.

"What's there to worry about?" I question him as I watch her obsessing over which dress would match Marcus's eyes better.

"Her crush over Marcus Thornberry, I mean, he obviously isn't a good guy to the both of us because we have eyes. Kaitlin on the other hand..."

"Maybe she'll be fine, I mean she did get one thing for certain, we don't entirely know him personally so we can't say anything yet. If he does end up breaking her, then we'll be there to help her pick up the pieces again." I mutter to Mack.

"Look at you," Mack knocks his shoulders with mine, "being all open-minded and stuff." He smiles down at me while I smile back up at him.

"Yeah, I've been trying it out recently. My therapist told me it would be good. And besides, it's just a silly little crush. I mean, I remember when you used to have a crush on me when I was younger." I knock his shoulder this time, smiling to myself as I walk away to another new rack.

"Yeah," Mack laughs, scratching the back of his neck, "used to."

"I just hope she's not completely head over heels for him." Mack goes to reply to me, but gets cut off by Kaitlin.

"Guys, I found the perfect color dress that matches Marcus's eyes! Isn't it just beautiful?!" Kaitlin holds the dress up to her torso, spinning around in it as the turquoise sequins fall all over her.

When I see Mack side eye me out of the corner of my eye, I realized I had gotten my answer.

She's completely head over heals in love and we'll, eventually, need to pick the fragments of her heart back up again.

Chapter 23: I Am Cinderella

"I still can't believe how much troublemakers those twins are," Kaitlin mutters as she hears Shiloh and Jacy crying from downstairs, "a couple months before their own due date, one of them punctures the very own sac they've been living in, causing Lavender to get tachycardia, thinking that she had a miscarriage."

"Can't you wait until we're older and are gonna have to babysit those fire starters." I grumble under my breath as I continue to sulk on top of my bed. Yes, being the oldest in family get togethers is not great at all.

"Hopefully, we'll be off for college before that happens." Kaitlin shivers at the thought, shaking a little bit of the bed with her. Suddenly, I hear an alarm go off, signaling Kaitlin's obnoxious scream. "Four hours and thirteen minutes left until the dance." Kaitlin stands on top of my bed, jumping up and down.

"Get down," I shoo her off with my hands, "I just fixed my bed!"

"You know what this means?! It's time for us to start getting ready!" Kaitlin jumps off of my bed and onto the floor, letting out a squeal and a little dance as she does so.

"That's a whole four hours, are you nuts?!" I glare at her as I turn on my stomach, planting my face into my pillow.

"Oh, just peanuts!" Kaitlin shouts as she grabs ahold of my leg, trying to slide me off of the bed. "Hurry up! We must perfect ourselves for tonight!"

"Why? So that we can live up to society's norms and be looked at and considered 'pretty'?" I manage to kick my foot out of Kaitlin's hold.

"Exactly! Duh!" Kaitlin goes to sit down in front of the vanity, unpacking all of the makeup that she brought over from her place. I watch as some makeup fall to the floor, finding no more space to sit on top of the vanity because it's all taken up.

"This room is as cluttered as it could ever be, I don't need you trying to make it worse." I sigh as I pick up a lipstick and hand it over to Kaitlin. "I can't believe it's Christmas Eve and I'm stuck here getting ready for a stupid dance." I kick the side of the bed, stubbing my toe on the metal frame. I instantly bring my foot up to hold, flopping on top of the bed. I grit my teeth as I squeeze my foot tighter, trying to ease the pain.

"Oh, sit down you big baby!" Kaitlin stands up from the chair, pointing at it for me to sit in it. I turn to glare at her from my place on the bed and hesitantly stand up, making my way back over to the vanity. I plop onto the seat and glare at all the makeup spread out in front of me, then I make eye contact with Kaitlin through the mirror and roll my eyes.

I watch Kaitlin cautiously as she picks up a big bottle, causing an avalanche to happen. "Close your eyes." Kaitlin says as she pops the top off of the bottle.

"Why would I need to close my ey-" Kaitlin interrupts me by spraying me in the face with the bottle, causing it to go in my mouth. I grab the inside of my shirt, wiping my tongue with it.

"Heehee..." Kaitlin smiles sheepishly as she holds up the bottle and shakes it, "primer spray."

"So, how does it feel?" Kaitlin comments as she backs away from my face, "admiring" her work.

I tilt my head from side to side very slowly, "It feels like I have twenty pounds sitting on my face."

"Good. That means I did something right." Kaitlin motions toward the mirror for me to take a look. I turn in the chair and face the mirror, checking out my new look for the night. "So?" Kaitlin squeals excitedly as she does a weird dance from the side of me.

I slightly shrug my shoulders at her, "It's good." I watch as Kaitlin's face drops into a frown.

"That's all that it gets?! Just a 'it's good'!" Kaitlin furrows her arms over her chest as she stares at me with a wild expression on her face. "You know in regular teen fictions the main character is supposed to be blown out of the water when she sees how her best friend helped her out for the school dance." I slightly raise my eyebrow at Kaitlin as she continues to rant on to me, "you're supposed to feel like Cinderella, like you're a whole new person...in a whole new world! Be ecstatic, snatch the boy of your dreams and have a happily ever after." Kaitlin dramatically runs up to me and practically shakes my shoulder out of its sockets, "Gosh darn it Ivory, we're running out of pages here! We're almost over!"

I hold up my index finger towards Kaitlin, "First of all, breathe." I watch as Kaitlin finally intakes a deep breath of air since her ranting begun. "Second, I don't see the big deal, I still look like a human being." Kaitlin narrows her eyes at me as she stands there not saying anything to me. With a flicker of her wrist, she shoo's me out of the chair with a groan.

"You're impossible." She sighs as she begins working on herself, quickly applying the products to her face. I sit on my bed, waiting until Kaitlin is finished when she stands up and does a twirl. "We're ready!" Kaitlin walks over to the bed as she takes my hand, dragging me over to the closet.

As we're opening the closet to reach for our dresses, we hear a voice from downstairs call out, "Mack's here!"

"Ugh, he always has to interrupt our fun." Kaitlin sighs dramatically as she shuts the closet door, opening it again very slowly to finally reveal our dresses. Kaitlin slowly drags out her baby blue dress with a sequined top and a long hampton skirt. I walk up and grab my simple red dress with an open leg, walking beside the vanity.

"You can change in the bathroom." I point towards the room, watching Kaitlin walk into it and shut the door behind her. Whew, here goes nothing. I quickly take my clothes off and slip into the dress easily. I step back into the middle of the room, in order to see my whole self in the reflection.

"Oh my god, I am Cinderella." Kaitlin shouts from behind the bathroom wall, making me shake my head as my curled hair falls around my face. I go back to sit on the bed once again as I fumble for my black heels. As I'm slipping my left foot into the heel, I hear a strange noise coming from the bedroom door.

"Don't mind me, I'm just crying because you're so grown up now!" Lavender covers her mouth with her hand as her eyes start to get watery. I simply roll my eyes at her as I continue to put the straps on. "And you are too!" I watch as Kaitlin flaunts out of the bathroom, one hand holding up her skirt as she waves it around. I hesitantly stand up and make my way over to Lavender and Kaitlin by the door.

"Oh my gosh, Ivory, look at you!" Kaitlin gushes as she pushes on my shoulder, sending me back a little.

"Come on you two, I think you made Mack wait long enough." Lavender is the first to leave the room with Kaitlin trailing behind her. I go to follow them when I quickly turn around, remembering to grab something. I walk over to my bed and reach into the back of the pillow, pulling out the replacement necklace that Mack had previously given me. I quickly put it on around my neck and fast walk out of the bedroom and into the living room.

I watch as everyone crowds around the bottom of the staircase, all conversing with each other in outside voices. As my heel makes contact with the first step, everyone stops their conversations, heads turning to look up at me in awe. The dramatics in this situation are not needed. I continue to bite the inside of my cheek as I watch Mack's face light up when he sees me coming down the stairs.

"Wow, Ivory, I just want to say that you look-you-I-I-" Mack gets cut off when Kaitlin cuts in, scooting to his side.

"Breathtakingly beautiful." Kaitlin sends me a wink and goes over to punch Kyle as he gushes over the way she looks tonight.

"Y-yes what Kaitlin said." Mack sheepishly smiles at me as he scratches the back of his neck. I tilt my head to the side as I notice something off about him.

"Can I?" I point towards his untidy tie and he looks down as a blush spreads over his cheeks. He quickly nods his head up and down and I undo the green tie, placing it correctly down on his neck and bring the two ends to the front as I easily tie them together. As I'm working on the tie, I decided to make light conversation with Mack. "You know I would always go into my fathers room when he wasn't looking, mostly because I was a troublemaker, but I enjoyed looking at all of the stuff adults got to dress in everyday. My father, one day, spotted me tied up with one of his ties and taught me how to tie them...he said incase my future husband didn't know how to or if I just ever wanted to wear one." As I'm done finishing the story, I place the tie down flat on top of Mack's chest, letting my hand linger there a bit longer than needed.

"I can easily imagine you tangled in your parents clothes." Mack chuckles a little bit as his lips turn upwards into a smile. "I see you're wearing the necklace." He motions towards my chest to wear the gold chain is hanging. "N-not that I was looking in that general direction towards you-" I quickly cut him off by holding my hand up.

"I get it. I'm really happy you gave this to me. Thank you again." I hold the chain in between my two fingers, playing with it as I keep my hand against my chest. Mack and I sit there for a few moments, smiling at each other before we get interrupted.

"All right, kiddos! It's time to gather around for pictures!" Lavender shouts as she holds up one of her photography cameras from work.

Chapter 24: Chanclas and Connections With The Italian Mafia

"Lavender, are you done taking photos yet?!" I groan at her for the millionth time as Kaitlin and Mack wonder the same thing in their heads. We have currently taken up an hour just for posing for Lavender's photos. If that's not the saddest thing I've ever said, I have no clue what is. All three of us are currently getting humiliated by the adults that are all currently surrounding us.

"You're done when I say you're done!" She shouts as the flash goes off, blinding the three of us in the process. I cross my arms over my chest as Lavender moves to a new position, getting a new angle.

"Do you hear that?" I pause and put my hand behind my ear for dramatic effect, "I think I hear the phone ringing from inside!" I point towards the house frantically.

"I don't hear any-" before Kaitlin can say anymore, I quickly jab her in her ribs.

"Oh, who cares. People call me everyday, they can wait a couple of minutes." Lavender huffs. More like an hour if she keeps this up.

"I'm pretty sure I heard the I.D. caller say 'Cherry and Sienna', your best friends!" I gasp, watching as Lavender hesitantly stands up. She looks over at me and raises her one eyebrow, then proceeds to walk to the house.

"Success! Nows our time to run!" I shout as I intertwine both of my arms with one of Mack's and Kaitlin's. I quickly run into the backseat of the closest car I see. Thankfully, it's my father and mothers car we ran into.

"Step on it, elderly people!" I shout to my dad, getting prepared to get slapped upside the head with a slipper by my mom. At least I'm directly behind her, she'd have a harder time reaching for me.

"No can do, kiddo," My father humors me as he holds up the car keys, "It seems I've lost my keys!" I groan out loud as I see Lavender step back outside of the house, searching for the three missing teenagers when she suddenly spots us in the car.

"Please, Dad!" I practically beg him, "my ankles hurt from standing in these neck-breakers for Lavender's photos!"

"Alright, alright, calmati!" He holds up his one hand as he turns the keys, turning on the car.

"Cariño, our daughter is both Italian and Latino, it's genetically impossible for her to calm down." My mother says from the passenger seat, putting her hand on my dads free hand.

"Stop! I need more pictures!" I hear Lavender shout at us from the grass, causing our mom to wave goodbye to her. I roll down my window as we pass her, sticking my tongue out at her as I send her a wink.

"We made a perfect family, didn't we?" My mom gives my dad goo-goo eyes, causing him to frantically look from the road to her.

"Sí, mi amor." My dad comments, causing mom to let out a toothey smile.

"Ti amo, cara mia." Mom smiles as they both slowly lean into each other, embracing each other with a kiss.

"Okay, ew!" I shout as I make gagging noises, covering my eyes with my hands, "it's bad enough that I have to see this, but my friends too!"

"This is why Violet was voted the least dramatic one in the family." I hear my mom mutter, pulling away from dad. "We're just around the corner, guys!" My mom mentions excitedly.

"You can time it down a couple more notches, it's not like it's prom." I mention to her as I look out of the window just as we pull up to the school.

"I'm not afraid to hit you with my chancla in front of your friends, keep that in the back of your mind." My mom makes eye contact with me through the side mirror, making me slowly slink in my seat. "You all look absolutely lovely tonight, I hope you have a divine time!"

"Thank you for the ride, Mr. and Mrs. Adeline!" Kaitlin and Mack say in unison, exiting the car with me trailing behind them before my mom stops me.

"Ivory, can we quickly talk to you for a second?" I stop dead in my tracks, motioning for Mack and Kaitlin to go on without me. I turn towards them both, waiting for them to speak.

"You do realize that we didn't send you over to Lavender's because...we 'didn't have time', right? It's just...I know how it feels to be the youngest in the family and have all of your siblings leave. It's tough and we were worried about you, you were slowly disconnecting from everyone and we though you'd be better off with Lavender. Especially knowing how close you two were with each other in the house." My mom says, waiting for my reaction. My confusion slowly slides into a smile and I nod my head at them. "She's smiling, I think there's still something wrong." My mom looks over at my dad worriedly.

"No, I mean, our family isn't exactly known for being subtle. I knew about that being the reasoning behind me getting sent to Lavender's. For that...I guess I'd like to thank you guys, not only for being wonderful parents who raised all of us wonderfully, but for knowing what's the best for us, thank you mom and dad." I quickly say as I watch my mom put a hand up to her heart, her eyes getting watery. I roll my eyes and climb into the backseat again, throwing my arms around both of them as they smother me with their old people cooties. Gosh, I really am turning into Lavender by the second.

"Now, get out! You don't wanna miss the whole dance because of us!" My mom shoos me out of the car and I step back with a laugh.

"And remember Ivory, no boys allowed. And if anyone tries to start any- thing with you, tell them your old man still has connections with the Italian mafia down in-" Before my dad can continue, I quickly cut him off.

"I'll make sure to use that piece of information on my resume when I become an FBI agent." I send them a small wave as I make my way around the car and into the school's gym. You've got to love the smell of jock strap at school dances. I quickly make my way over to Mack and Kaitlin when I spot them standing besides the bleachers.

"There. Marcus Thornberry." Kaitlin sighs as she writes his name in cursive letters on top of an envelope. "Whew. I'm nervous! Someone tell me I'm not gonna get my heart broken tonight!" Kaitlin turns around and looks both Mack and I in our eyes.

"Don't look at me." I hold my hands up defensively, watching Kaitlin squint her eyes at me, quickly turning towards Mack.

"Do you hear that? I also think that I hear my home phone ringing." Mack mutters as Kaitlin grumbles under her breath, rolling her eyes at us.

"It's fine! It doesn't matter, all I want to do is get this confession off of my chest and have fun for the rest of the night." Kaitlin closes her eyes and takes a deep breath, then reopens them again with determination in them. "Here goes nothing." Kaitlin ungracefully runs up to the booth, shoving her card into the box.

"Let's cross our fingers so everything can work out perfectly." Mack sheepishly smiles as I see his fingers cross over one another.

"Unlikely." I whisper as I also cross my own.

Chapter 25: Work On Your Hiding Skills

"So, are we just gonna sit here...standing behind this fake plant as we try and fail at listening to Kaitlin and Marcus' conversation?" Mack asks, ducking his head every time he sees either one of their heads move towards our general direction.

"That's exactly what we're going to do." I nod my head up and down, holding onto Mack's shoulder to peer over the plant and watch them. Kaitlin and Mack were currently on the "date" that the student council had set up as a "fun activity" in order to improve the relationship between students. Whatever that meant. Kaitlin had used hers on Marcus, a boy who she barely even knows and somehow she managed to fall completely head over heels for him.

You'd probably call us bad friends for not trying to talk Kaitlin out of doing this because it's obvious how this is gonna end; Marcus will break her heart. However, Kaitlin's just one of those people who will not take your advice no matter what you say, she'll just have to learn on her own.

After the student council had to basically drag Marcus to Kaitlin, they've been sat there for around ten minutes or so...just talking. Which in this case was very suspicious. Marcus did not earn the nickname 'thorn heart' for no reason.

"How do you think it's going?" I whisper to Mack, still holding onto him as we both peer out from the plant.

"I'm not sure, we can't exactly hear from this far of a distance." Mack shrugs his shoulder, pulling us back behind the plant again. Mack stares at me for a little while longer before I raise my eyebrow at him.

"Is there something on my face." I respond to him more as a statement than a question.

"N-no." I notice a tinge of pink rise to his cheeks. "Ivory, there's something I need to-"

"Ivory?" Now that's a voice I wasn't expecting to hear tonight. I turn around and see Shelby standing there, awkwardly shifting from one foot to the other. "Can we talk?" Talk...? About what?

"Sure." I nod my head up and down, following her as she goes to a more secluded side of the gym. I suddenly turn around, sending Mack a shrug as he looks at me with wide eyes. Shelby suddenly stops, lacing her fingers together as she looks up at me and starts speaking.

"First off, I wanna say that I'm sorry...I-I never would've flirted with Zayne if I actually knew he was taken, I want to let you know that I am not one of those girls. I also know about your guys little fight and all of that...so, I wanted to let you know that if you feel uncomfortable with me starting a relationship with Zayne or if you change your mind and still have feelings for him, I'll totally back down and you can have him all to yourself. I just want to know that I never meant to hurt you." Shelby quickly rushes out and I furrow my eyebrows down at her.

"Shelby, I currently hold nothing against you, I don't blame you for anything that had happened. Sure, I did feel a little upset and jealous because Zayne was spending all of his time with you and I knew he liked you so much more than he ever liked me, but I never blamed you for something you didn't even know in the first place." I stop and let her process my words before I continue speaking, "If you honestly like Zayne you should tell him how you feel and make your relationship with him official. I can tell he really likes you too." I send her a small smile that makes her face fully brighten up.

"Really?! You really think so?!" Shelby asks me excitedly and I release a laugh as I nod my head up and down. Shelby unexpectedly pulls me into a bone crushing hug, causing all of the oxygen to be released from my body. What a breath-taker. Literally. "Thank you, Ivory." Shelby says to me one last time before heading off to the dance floor with some of her friends. I fast-walk my way back to Mack, filling him in on what just currently happened.

"You're a really nice person, Ivory." Mack informs me wholeheartedly, making me widen my eyes up at him.

"Nice?" I question him.

"You're a good person. I'm being serious, not a lot of girls would have done the same thing you just did. You don't let pettiness come first."

"You better stop filling my ego up. Pretty soon it's gonna be the size of this whole gym!" I warn Mack and watch as he laughs and shakes his head. "Uh-oh, look, twelve o'clock." Mack points at Kaitlin who's currently walking our way with anger written all over her face.

"How was your date?" Mack asks her as soon as she comes up to us.

"I don't know. Why don't you answer that, it seemed like you two were more involved in the conversation than I was." Kaitlin crosses her arms in front of her chest, looking back and forth between Mack and I.

"Kaitlin, we were just worried about you." I say, watching her anger slowly dissolve.

"I know, I know. I'm just sayin, if you goofus's ever want to be secret agents, you'll have to work on your hiding skills a lot more."

"How bad was it?" Mack asks as he sheepishly smiles.

"Let's just say that if this was a mission, you'd have been assassinated in point five seconds."

"Yikes. I guess we've gotta hand in our badges, Ivory." Mack sadly pouts at me, making me frown.

"Aww, but the dental insurance was so good." I let my head hang lowly, allowing my hair to fall in front of my face.

"You two should be actors." Kaitlin points at Mack and I, causing Mack and I to look at each other.

We quickly shake our heads in disapproval as we both say, "nah", in unison.

"I bet you're all waiting for me to answer the billion dollar question." Kaitlin looks over the two of us as Mack leans over and whispers in my ear.

"All?" He looks around, furrowing his eyebrows when he sees no one else standing around us.

"Marcus said he had no interest being more than a slight acquaintance to me, so that's that." Kaitlin shrugs her shoulders.

"Are you okay?" I ask her, reaching out to put my hand on top of her shoulder.

"Yeah, I'm fine. Honestly, it could've gone a lot worse than how it did go down." She answers for me.

"Are you sure you're okay because- to me, it feels like world war three is about to happen." Mack gives Kaitlin a once-over, making sure that she is okay and not lying.

"Gosh, I'm not a child. I'm not gonna cry about something I knew was gonna happen all along. I did it for myself, I was gonna put myself out there for love and if it didn't work out, fine, I'll just move on. No more wasting time." Kaitlin informed us, making me agree with her in approval.

"Well, I'm really proud that you did that for yourself, Kaitlin." I smile at her, sending a quick wink her way.

"Now, it's time to finally live up to this title and dance." Kaitlin shouts as she pumps her fists in the air to the music, making her way to the dance floor. I'm about to follow her when I get pulled back once again, Mack holding onto my wrist lightly.

"Before we do that, can we talk?" Mack scratches the back of his neck, signaling his nervousness. What is it with people and wanting to talk to me this night. I motion with my hand for him to continue and he does so. "I don't actually know if you knew all along about this because in my opinion I thought I was being obvious or maybe, you didn't notice at all and maybe you're more oblivious than Lavender, but Ivory I've had a crush on you...for the longest time. I've tried so hard to bury it under and get rid of it in order to preserve our friendship and keep it in tact, but it's been taking a toll on me recently. We're growing up, we're not kids anymore and I thought this should be a good time to tell you."

I sit there and intake his words slowly. I go to open my mouth and comment, before getting cut off by Mack again, "Y-you don't have to say or do anything you don't want to. I wasn't actually expecting anything to be said in return." Mack tries to turn and walk away before I grab his hand, tugging him back towards me.

"Mack, you know how much I care for you, I love you. And, because of that...I don't want to end up hurting you in the process. Not only did I just get over a pretty useless and bad relationship not that long ago, but I still need to learn how to love myself in order to properly love someone else. I'm not gonna try and speak for the future, but we'll possibly see what happens until then. And if we find others before then, then so be it."

"I know that I'm the one who brought up all the mushy and deep stuff, but now it's really starting to kill the vibe. I appreciate your honesty, Ivory, that's just one of the many traits that I love about you. And until the future comes up, let's get our booties on the dance floor and do what we know best!" Mack shouts as he reaches for my hand, tugging me towards the dance floor with him. I let out a laugh as the three of us dance around each other, blending and mixing in with the crowd that's surrounding us.

I, Ivory-Lynn Daisy Adeline, was not able to tell the future. Unfortunately.

I also cannot tell you if the 'Adeline high school soulmate blessing' was true or not.

But what I can tell you is that I intended for my high school soulmate to be myself. I have my goal and my deadline set. Before senior year of high school, I will learn to accept myself who I am wholeheartedly and fall in love with me.

And whenever the right one comes along, or maybe he already did, I'll make sure to snatch them up at an appropriate time.

Something my family does not know the meaning of.

Until then, however, I will continue to go on with my life, surrounded by my crazy friends and family who I know will always have my back when I need it.

But you probably already knew all of that already. Wanna know one thing that I can tell you though?

For the rest of the night, we danced like there was no tomorrow.

But there was, we all knew there was...because the ending is only the beginning.

(\(•~•)/)

Christmas Special!

One year later.

I was currently on the balcony, looking down at everyone who was currently arriving. The Adeline's have been known to succumb to the 'fashionably late' belief and it truly showed. It was four p.m.- not only was everyone asked to show up at two, but they were also asked to wear ugly sweaters. Looks like they listened to neither.

"Typical Adeline's." I grumble out loud, continuing to watch them pile into the house.

"Are you planning everyone's demise?" A small voice asks from behind me and I turn around to see the weird six year old watching me.

"No, Jezabel, I'm not." I inform her.

"The apocalypse?"

"Uhm, no."

"The overtake of the government?"

"No. I'm just sitting here, watching people," I motion my hand out to all the cars parking and pulling up.

"Seems highly unlikely." She squints her eyes at me as she gives me a once-over. Jezabel slowly comes to my side, sitting on the chair next to me. "Great-grandpa smells like eggs."

I throw my head back as I practically become one with my chair. As you can tell, I really didn't want to deal with all the drama of the family visiting. "He's old." I inform her politely, dragging my hand down my face.

"You're old and you don't smell like eggs." She sticks her small index finger at me, holding tightly onto her stuffed reindeer with her other hand.

"I'm not old." I cross my arms over my chest as I stare at Jezabel.

"Whatever helps you sleep at night," Jezabel shrugs her shoulders at me. Wow, I'm arguing with a six year old- cross that off of my bucket list.

"Come on," I suddenly stand up, holding out my hand for Jezabel to take- which she does. As we head outside of the room, I spot Sterling and Shy in the hallway looking suspicious. "And what are you two up to?"

"Nothing!" Sterling shouts, crouching down to loudly whisper 'sshh' into Shy's ear. I widen my eyes as I suddenly hear a loud crash coming from the room across from us.

"What is this sticky substance?!" Someone shouts and I quickly grab Sterling's hand, while he holds onto Shy's.

"Alright, that's enough trouble you two are gonna create tonight." I suddenly hear the door unlocking and hurriedly whisper to the three of them, "Now, it's time for a fun game I'd like to call run!" I lightly shout as we all take-off, rushing off behind the corner just as soon as the person comes out of the bathroom. As we're rushing down the hall, we quickly stumble into someone.

"Move!" I shout as I try to step out around her, but she quickly pulls me back with ease. I huff and let go of the kids hands, watching them all run off.

"Is that the kind of welcome I get from my own sister?" She says incredulously as I sit there catching my breath for a second.

"As you can hear, I'm not really able to give you the proper welcome that you want." I get muffled with fabric as she bring me in close for a hug. "Why are you so emotional? Are you pregnant too? Pretty soon I'm gonna be the last Adeline child that isn't pregnant." I mutter into her shirt as she continues to hold me tightly.

"Very funny, Ivory. Sage isn't pregnant." Violet points out as she finally releases me from her hold.

Sage and Michael had finally started to settle down and with settling down comes children. Only one thing though, they were a gay couple and, unfortunately, they were not able to create their own child. However, they could adopt and that is exactly what they're doing. They already have their eyes set on a certain kid that both of them refuse to tell anyone else about because they want it to be a surprise.

"Yes, but that doesn't stop me from making the pregnant jokes about him." I wink at her as I elbow her, then stop when I finally notice something. "Wait, you didn't deny that you weren't pregnant."

"Oh my god, I'm not pregnant, Ivory." Violet rolls her eyes at me as I steadily look at her. I quickly punch her in her left breast, causing her to double over. "What was that for?!" She grits out through her teeth.

"Well, when you're pregnant, your boobs are very sensitive. Looking at the reaction you just made, I'm gonna go out on a gut feeling and say that you are."

"You punched me in the tit! I'm pretty sure I'm allowed to feel pain!" She continues to hold her left breast, coming back up. "I'm not pregnant!" She hisses at me as she punches me back in my boob.

"Ouch." I mutter as I cross my arms over my chest, protecting my sack of fats.

"Oh, you have working pain receptors, Ivory?! I think that means you're pregnant!" Violet jabs her finger in my chest, causing me to stagger back a little bit.

I squint my eyes at her, "You little-"

"Pregnant?!" I hear someone from behind Violet shout, causing me to look over her and see our mom standing there with a ludicrous look on her face. Violet sheepishly smiles, turning around to face our mom.

"Hey, mom," Violet sends her a small wave as mom squint her eyes at me.

"Pregnant?" She repeated again in a harder tone.

"Before you say anything else, just know that Violet is out of her damn mind! I'm not pregnant!" I quickly rush out to her, but her face still remains the same.

"Watch your mouth." Is all she says as she juts her hip out. Give it up to mothers who care more about the language their child is using than actually listening to the context of what they're saying. "Ivory-Lynn, you better hope for your own sake and for Mack's that you're not pregnant. I love that dear boy like family, but if you're carrying his child right now-"

I blur out the rest of the words as I hear Violet speaking besides me, "Wow, I forgot just how scary mom was. I'm not even the one getting scolded and I feel like I've done something wrong."

"That's because you did, idiot!" I whisper harshly to her. "You're turning violet, Violet." I mutter to her, knowing that I'm getting on her nerves.

"Shut up." She groans as we both refocus our attention on our mom.

"-And then, I'll hide your bodies in the depths of the Mariana Trench-"

"Mom, I was just joking around with Ivory, alright? She's not pregnant." Violet finally spits out as I breathe in relief.

"Besides, Mack and I haven't done that stuff." I inform both of them as my mom practically beams at me.

"Aww, my little mija, so innocent!" Mom laughs as she pinches my left cheek.

"Alright, alright, hands off of the merchandise." I shoo her off of me as I continue to walk past them and down the stairs. I feel myself slowing down when I notice how many people are packed in the living room.

"Can you believe them? They have the nerve to be late and they turn around and complain that the tree isn't properly decorated?" Someone's shoulder knocks with my own, sending me stumbling. Just as I'm about to trip on my face, the person grabs me and puts me upright again. As soon as I'm standing on my feet, the person traps me in their arms and gives me a nuggy. "Come on! I thought I taught you better than this! If someone puts you in a chokehold, you jab them in their eyes so they'll release."

"I know aunt Elvira, I just don't want to hurt you." She finally releases me from her hold and puts her hand on my head, ruffling my hair.

"Please, as if a tiny thing your size would be able to hurt me." She was right about one thing. Aunt Elvira is a strange woman who stands at around six foot one and on her skates for roller derby, she grows another three or four inches. Aunt Elvira is apart of the tolerable group of the family, ever since I was little I envied how she always made any situation fun.

"Say that again when you're old and walking around in a cane." I narrow my eyes, looking up to her with a smirk on my face.

"You're on!" She holds out her hand for me to shake to which I comply.

"Where's uncle Alejandro?" I look around, noticing the absence of her husband. Uncle Alejandro, also apart of the tolerable group.

"He's out back still trying to impress, grandpa." She shakes her head, making her natural curls fall over her shoulder. Ah, yes, my mom and my aunt's father was a very unpleasant person to be around and even though everyone agreed on that statement, people have yet to say anything. Not only does he have a nasty attitude, but like Jezabel said, he smells like eggs.

"Do you think I have a chance of ignoring him throughout this whole day?" I hesitantly ask her.

"Not a chance, muñeca."

Rats.

"Why not?!"

"Because it's supposed to be a surprise."

"Fine. Then, I won't stop making pregnant jokes about you." I send him my most intimidating glare.

"Why did I have to be born the only boy?" I hear Sage sighs before sitting, backing down. Even though I was almost eighteen, I still have not lost my streak of being a nuisance. Since Lavender has had gotten children and gotten a bit mature, I have temporarily taken on her roll of being the family meddler. My current task at hand was figuring out Sage and Michael's kid.

"So, it's gonna be a boy, isn't it?"

"Until you stop asking questions about her, I'm gonna ignore you." Sage doesn't realize the slip of his tongue and I smile in satisfaction.

"Hey, Michael-"

"No, Ivory, I'm not as dumb as Sage, I'm not gonna reveal anything about our child." Michael quickly shuts me down and I nod my head up and down.

"Fair enough." Hearing my stomach grumble, I quickly stand up from the couch and make my way towards the kitchen in search for some food.

As I step closer to the kitchen I see a familiar redhead and a insert what you call people with black hair. I see Cherry, Sienna, and Lavender all huddled in a circle in the middle of the kitchen, gossiping and giggling like teenagers.

"Please move, plebeians." I shoo them out of the way as I open the fridge, looking around for candy.

"Ivory! I was wondering when you'd finally come out of your dark cave!" Lavender says as she turns and faces me.

"I hope grandpa hugs you." I say to her as I settle on a snickers bar and a yogurt.

"How dare you!" Lavender gasps loudly, looking insulted, "that's a horrible thing to say to someone!" Lavender quickly knocks on wood, practically begging that it won't happen. I reach into the drawer, pulling out a spoon and plop it into my mouth. "Hi Cherry, Sienna," I send them both a small wave and they do the same.

"Stop trying to brainwash my friends, overgrown rat!" You know what I said about Lavender being a bit mature, I take it back. I quickly roll my eyes at Lavender and sit in the kitchen with the three of them while I eat my yogurt. I refuse to venture back out there with food in my hands, one of those vultures are bound to smell it and try and steal it away from me. I'm not doubting my abilities, I know if they tried anything with me I'd be able to easily win them, I just didn't have the energy to do it today.

I overhear the three adults conversation, "I always thought that Cherry would be the one to have fifty children first." Sienna says honestly with Cherry bobbing her head up and down at her.

"Yeah, me too." Cherry agrees with her, not really understanding Sienna's true meaning behind the words.

"Well, when it happens it happens." Lavender shrugs her shoulders, continuing to focus on frosting the cupcakes. Honestly, I don't blame Lavender for having quite a few kids even this early in her life. With girls having periods and all, I'd take any chance that I can get in order to not get that red demon every month. Maybe not every chance right now, but you know what I mean. I hear the doorbell ring and I hurriedly rush towards the door, opening it wide to see Kaitlin and Kyle standing there with many gifts in their arms.

Kaitlin and Kyle's side of the family didn't have enough time to come to our house this year for Christmas because they were currently on their way visiting in-laws, but they still managed to get every single one of us gifts and send us heartfelt letters. Cherry was supposed to go with them, seeing as she is their cousin, but didn't want to make the hassle of going back and forth.

"Are those all for me? You shouldn't have!" Lavender teases her husband, putting her hand over her heart.

"You know it." He sends her a small wink and I close the door behind them as they enter.

"Wow, a Christmas miracle, my cousins finally doing work for once!" Cherry claps excitedly as she watches Kyle and Kaitlin struggle with the million boxes in their hands.

"Thanks for the support, grape." Kyle grumbles as he rushes to the tree, quickly placing all of the presents down.

"I. Am. Miserable!" Kaitlin huffs as she dumps all of the presents on the floor. "Oops, that didn't sound too good. Hopefully these presents have the receipts in them." She smiles sheepishly as she picks the presents up again, handing some to me to take and place under the tree with her.

"Have you heard from Mack yet?" Kaitlin asks me as she sits on the flor next to the tree, stretching out her legs and arms.

"Sadly, no. His mom has him on lockdown until six, after they finish opening presents." I sigh as I sit down next to her.

"It's funny how you constantly said the two of us were flirting when we were fighting, look how the tables have turned." Kaitlin does a wave with her eyebrows, trying to smirk at me, failing.

I quickly laugh at her facial expression, "Please, never make that face ever again, that is nightmare fuel." I inform her as she starts to laugh too.

"You know what would be fun? If we all watched Krampus." Kaitlin smiles evilly as I facepalm myself, shaking my head.

"You really wanna traumatize the children, don't you?"

"Hey, I'll take any chance I can get! Those little suckers ruined my favorite lipstick!" Kaitlin pouts once again.

"Maybe later we can go shopping and get you a new favorite." I throw the idea out there and watch as Kaitlin's face droops.

"Lipsticks are not like humans, they're non-replaceable." Kaitlin sadly shakes her head and I roll my eyes at her.

"You're nuts, I hope you realize this."

Some of the family is currently sat on the couch, watching movies while the rest- or should I say practically all the boys are outside watching football in the garage.

"Ugh, I think Shiloh had an accident." Kaitlin suddenly plugs her nose, holding Shiloh at an arms distance away from her.

Cherry, sitting besides Kaitlin, holding Jacy, also plugs her nose. "Jacy did too." I quickly tuck my nose under my shirt and slowly scoot away from the two girls in order to not smell the stinky babies.

The doorbell suddenly rings, causing me to stand up and practically run towards the door while everyone groans at me for blocking the screen for one second. I excitedly throw the door open, beaming up at him.

"Thank god you're here, I cannot take one more second of my family and their stinky diapers." I quickly inform him as I hold the door open for him to step in.

"Glad to be of assistance." He laughs as he takes off his shoes by the door.

"Come on, I wanna show you something." I don't wait for him to reply and grab his hand, tugging him along with me upstairs and into the guest bedroom. I quickly pull back the curtains and open the sliding door, revealing the beautiful sky. "We made it, just in time." I breath out as I smile out across at the breathtaking scenery.

"Wow, it's amazing." Mack smiles as he also steps out onto the balcony besides me, staring at the multicolored sunset. I slightly nod my head up and down, agreeing with him as I reach for his hand, holding it in my own. I watch out of the corner of my eye as Mack looks down at our intertwined hands, smiling to himself.

I feel my cheeks unexpectedly heat up and turn pink. I turn my head slightly away, hiding my blush with my hair. Mack and I have been going out with each other for eight months now and I know that we're still way too early in our relationship to say anything, but I hope that we last for a really long time.

I really like him and he makes me feel proud and happy to be myself- this is the first time in my life where I can say that I'm happy that I was born into this world and I'm happy that I'm in my own comfortable skin right now with one of the many people who opened my eyes to see just how important I am. I have also come to term with my O.D.D, that it was going nowhere and neither was I. I still have a lot to learn about it and my therapist says I'm improving really well.

Other than that, I have learned that my mental illness does not define me as who I am.

"Hey, would you look at that," Mack exclaims, making me turn my head to face his completely. He points above our heads to where a mistletoe is hanging peacefully. Huh, that wasn't there before.

I look around us cautiously, trying to find the person who could've placed it there, but find no one.

"I guess we have no choice but to kiss each other now." Mack shrugs, trying hard to contain his smile.

"Aww, do I have to?" I pout up to him, making him bust out into a full smile. Mack rests his hand on my cheek as I stand up on my tip toes in order to match his full height.

And for the rest we laughed and danced the night away.

And this is how the girl with the bad attitude was able to learn to love herself and others around her.